DARK WATERS

Raintree is an imprint of Capstone Global Library Limited, a company incorporated in England and Wales having its registered office at 264 Banbury Road, Oxford, OX2 7DY – Registered company number: 6695582

www.raintree.co.uk
myorders@raintree.co.uk

Edited by Julie Gassman
Designed by Hilary Wacholz
Illustrated by Kirbi Fagan
Production by Tori Abraham
Printed and bound in China

ISBN 978-1-4747-3399-1 (paperback)
21 20 19 18 17
10 9 8 7 6 5 4 3 2 1

British Library Cataloguing in Publication Data
A full catalogue record for this book is available from the British Library.

THE SIGHTING

A MERMAID'S JOURNEY

by JULIE GILBERT
illustrated by KIRBI FAGAN

a Capstone company — publishers for children

PREFACE

My name is India Finch. People say it's a funny name. India is a country, and a finch is a kind of bird. A country and a bird. It's an odd name for someone who is a mermaid. Well, part mermaid.

Confused? Me too. I didn't know I was part-mermaid until this summer. I'm spending the summer with my grandpa on the coast of Cornwall. It's beautiful here. Lots of Cornish palms trees, harbours and beaches. And the ocean is amazing. The sea stretches forever and ever. The waves crash against the rocks.

The ocean makes me feel huge and small at the same time. It feels like home.

I was shocked when Grandpa told me he was part-mer. I thought he was joking. Turns out he wasn't. Grandpa's mother was a mermaid. He's part-mer, and so am I.

On the outside, I look like an ordinary girl. I have medium brown skin, dark brown eyes and crinkly dark hair. I get my stubborn chin from my mum and my crooked ears from my dad. I'm tall for my age, and my arms and legs are strong.

I look like an ordinary girl in the water too. When I'm in the ocean, I don't grow a tail or gills. But salt water makes my mer abilities wake up. I can breathe water instead of air. I can also swim for miles and miles without getting tired. And I can use my hands to heal injuries and illnesses. I have extra powers because I'm female. All mermaids have powers, but none of the mermen do.

My mermaid friends have amazing powers too.

Nari can talk to sea creatures using her mind. She can communicate with fish and lobsters and seals.

She says the sea creatures make better friends than most of the mer.

Dana can make water thick. When she does, I feel as if I'm swimming in clear jelly. She likes to tease us sometimes. We'll be swimming along, and suddenly the water is too thick to move.

Lulu can move currents and make waves. She's really strong, just like her personality. I shouldn't have favourites, but I like Lulu the best. She's a fighter, like me. Or at least how I want to be.

The mer used to live all over the oceans. That's why so many cultures have stories about mermaids, even though people don't believe in them. It's funny that humans don't know the mer are real. Humans are to blame for so many mer problems, after all.

Mer homes have always been protected by domes. The domes are like giant snow globes that make whatever is inside them invisible. The dome forms naturally when the mer live in harmony with their surroundings. Once people started drilling for oil, laying cables and polluting oceans, mer homes were destroyed. The domes protecting the mer collapsed.

The mer started to die out. The remaining mer banded together and formed two tribes. Even though the tribes don't always get along, the mer are safer together than apart.

Almost three hundred mer live in two tribes in the deep underwater valleys called canyons off the coast of Cornwall. My mermaid friends are part of the Ice Canyon tribe. The other tribe is the Fire Canyon tribe. Neither tribe likes humans.

The Ice Canyon tribe wants to leave the humans alone. Live and let live, they say. The Fire Canyon mer are different. They want to attack humans and punish them.

Members from the different tribes aren't supposed to hang out with each other. This means I can't spend as much time with Evan as I'd like to. He's one of the Fire Canyon mer. He's also really smart – and cute. He seems to like me too.

I don't know how long I'll be able to hang out with Evan or any of my friends. Grandpa told me that when he was a young man, he had to choose between living on land or in the sea.

He had fallen in love with my grandmother. She was human. Because of her, Grandpa chose land. But he promised that his children and grandchildren would always help the mer.

Unfortunately my dad wanted nothing to do with the mer. He used to swim with them when he was my age, but then something happened. Dad made a bad decision, and a mermaid died. I don't know the whole story and neither does Grandpa.

When he was old enough, Dad moved to the West Midlands. Grandpa said Dad wanted to keep me away from the ocean while I was growing up. As a kid, I never knew I was part-mer. But I think Dad wanted me to know. Right before I got on the train, Dad took me by the shoulders.

"Trust Grandpa," he said. "Whatever he says. No matter how crazy it sounds."

Then he hugged me tight and walked away.

I didn't know what Dad meant until I came to Cornwall and discovered my mer abilities. I still don't know if my mum knows. Even if Dad told her, I'm not sure she'd believe him.

The first time I talked with Dad on the phone, I asked him about the mer. I told him how shocked I was to learn the news. And that I wanted to know everything.

"We'll talk about it when you get home," was all he said.

I like being with the mer. They call me when they need my help by sending a seaweed wreath. Then I jump into the ocean to be with my friends.

Because I'm half-human, the dome makes it impossible for me to find the canyons on my own. The canyons are invisible to me until I'm fully inside the dome.

My human eyes can't see the dome, either, although it's supposed to be beautiful. My friends have to take me to and from the canyons where the mer live.

We have lots of wild adventures. Sometimes, though, I wonder if the mer only like me because of my powers. After all, I'm the only one who has healing powers. Would they even want me around if I couldn't help them?

I also wonder what my future holds. Will I have to make the same choice Grandpa did? Will I have to choose between my human side and my mermaid side? I'm not sure. I don't know which side I'd pick.

Maybe one day I'll know for sure.

CHAPTER 1

I don't like marshmallows. They remind me of the yearly camping trips our school makes us go on. On the last evening, we always have a big bonfire. Everyone rushes to shove their marshmallows in the fire. Except me. Marshmallows are sticky and gross. Especially when they are toasted.

So when we got to the beach and Grandpa tossed me a bag of marshmallows, I was cranky.

"Your dad's favourite," he said.

"Not mine," I replied under my breath.

I dug through the carrier bags. Grandpa had packed carrot sticks and vegetable Cornish pasties. No chocolate or sweets, though ... not even any crisps or a piece of fruit.

Now, two hours later, I'm still hungry. I pick up a marshmallow and toss it into the fire. I'm not sure where Grandpa went. He strolled down the beach half an hour ago. I haven't seen him since.

The marshmallow starts to ooze and turn black. I toss another one in and watch it do the same. I throw in a third.

This is the most fun I've had all week.

I know I'm cranky because I'm in Cornwall and not at home with my friends. I don't mind Cornwall. It's actually nice. I'd never been here before this summer. The ocean is amazing. I could listen to the waves forever. I've got to know Grandpa. And there are my mermaid friends.

My heart lurches.

Even though it is getting dark, I peer at the shoreline. Maybe today I'll see a wreath of seaweed.

My mermaid friends send a wreath when they need my help. Trouble is, they haven't summoned me for a few weeks. I'm not supposed to swim to them on my own, either. They live in a place called Ice Canyon, which is protected by a magical dome. The dome makes Ice Canyon invisible to humans. Even though I'm part-mer, my eyes are too human. I can't see the dome. If I tried to swim to Ice Canyon, I'd never find it.

I try to keep busy. I visit the library in town most days. But it's so small that I've already read almost everything. I walk along the beach each morning, picking up litter. Sometimes I volunteer at the museum where Grandpa works. Today I sorted fishing hooks for an exhibit, which was pretty dull but better than nothing.

I miss my friends.

The marshmallow bag sits by my hip. I toss another marshmallow into the flames.

"Don't waste food, India," Grandpa says. His brown skin looks even darker in the shadows.

"Sorry," I say.

“Not a marshmallow fan, I see,” Grandpa says.

“Not really,” I say.

“Next time we have a bonfire, you can buy the groceries,” Grandpa says. He settles on the sand across from me. The fire is burning low. Soon it will be nothing but hot, white ash.

“Where did you go?” I ask.

“Just went for a walk, India,” he says.

“Did you ... did you find anything?” I ask, a note of hope in my voice.

“You mean a seaweed wreath?” Grandpa asks.

I nod, not sure he can see me in the shadows.

“No,” he says.

I shrug. “It’s just that I haven’t seen any of my mermaid friends in a while,” I say. “I miss them.” An image of Lulu, Dana and Nari floats through my mind.

“I’m sure they miss you too,” Grandpa murmurs.

“Was it like this for you?” I ask. “Back when you used to swim with the mer?”

I don't expect Grandpa to answer. He doesn't talk much about his time with the mer. I know he used to swim with them when he was a boy. When he got older, he fell in love with my grandmother. It was too hard to have both a mer family and a human one, he said. So he picked. He chose my grandmother.

"They didn't need me like they need you," Grandpa says, surprising me.

"Why not?" I ask.

"You have powers," he says. "I didn't."

"Oh, yeah," I say. Only mermaids have powers, not mermen. "What kinds of adventures did you have with them?"

Grandpa sighs and stretches his legs towards the fire. He moves slowly, as if his knees are giving him trouble. Sometimes I forget how old he is.

"Truth be told, India, I never spent too much time with the mer," he says.

"You didn't?" I ask. I'm surprised to hear this. He's always talking so much about how the mer are family. I just assumed he had spent a lot of time beneath the waves.

"When I was a boy, I had a few mer friends who would meet me by the rocks," Grandpa says. "Those same rocks where you meet your friends."

"Oh, right," I say, picturing the jagged black rocks that jut into the ocean. The tides are dangerous for humans, but when I jump into the water my mer abilities take over, and I'm fine.

"We spent long summer days together," Grandpa says, his voice growing tender. "We used to race up and down the shoreline. Sometimes we'd swim further into the sea to play with the dolphins. But they never took me to the canyons."

"Why not?" I ask.

"The canyons were new," Grandpa says. "Most of the mer were still living scattered across the oceans at the time. My friends were some of the first mer to live in the canyons. The mer elders didn't want them bringing me to their new home. I was too human."

"I know the feeling," I say, thinking about the dirty looks I get when I visit the canyons. The Ice Canyon mer don't always like me, even though I'm only there to help.

"The mer have always been worried about humans," Grandpa says. "Humans are the ones who polluted the oceans, after all. If the waters were still clean, the mer would be able to live anywhere."

"The waters around here aren't always clean," I point out. "Whenever I swim, I find plastic bottles and carrier bags and oil slicks. So what makes the canyons so special?"

Grandpa clears his throat, a low gurgling sound. "They're not," he says. "There's nothing unique about the canyons."

"Why do the mermaids all live there, then?" I ask.

"Many years ago, the mer realized their numbers were shrinking. Probably because of pollution. Or perhaps it is simply time for the mer to die out," Grandpa explains.

"I don't believe that," I protest. I don't want to think about a world where there are no mermaids.

"I don't believe that, either," Grandpa says. "Whatever the reason, mer tribes from all over agreed to live together for protection. The canyons were a good place to hide."

"They are," I confirm, thinking of the massive cliffs rising from the ocean floor. "Why do you like the mer so much if they never even took you to the canyons?"

"They are family," Grandpa barks.

He always says this when I talk about the mer. Grandpa is always talking about how we need to be loyal to the mer and help them. I'm starting to think the relationship isn't balanced. The mer get more from us than we get from them.

"Why should we always be the ones helping the mer? Why can't we just hang out with them sometimes?" I ask.

"You've been to the canyons," Grandpa says. "Would they let you simply hang out with them?"

"Well, no," I say. "But we don't get anything out of the relationship. Not really."

Grandpa gazes at me. "We are part-mer. It is our heritage. Like how you are both African-Caribbean and white," he says. "You must understand where you are from. Only then can you understand who you are."

"Huh," I say. I am proud that I'm biracial. Being part-mer is not quite the same, although I understand what Grandpa is saying. He wants me to explore what it means for me to be mer. For him, it means loyalty and family. I'm not sure what it means to me yet.

"Do you wish you could see the canyons?" I ask, changing the subject slightly. I trace a pattern on the cool sand with my fingers.

Grandpa coughs and clears his throat again. "I'm too old for wishing," he says. He is shutting down our conversation. He rises to his feet and kicks sand over the dying embers. "Time to go home," he says.

"I'll be there in a minute," I say. "I want to look at the stars."

Grandpa watches me for a moment before he shrugs. "Suit yourself. I'll leave you a torch."

"Thanks," I say.

When he's gone, I look towards the ocean, not the stars. I pace the beach. I search for a wreath that doesn't exist. Will my friends ever summon me just to hang out? Or do they only need me when there's a problem?

I shiver and wrap my arms around myself. The waves shush against the sand. The stars arch overhead, cold and distant.

"Where are you guys?" I whisper. A breeze stirs over the water, whisking my question away.

I'm all alone. I turn the torch on and return to Grandpa's cottage.

CHAPTER 2

"Catch the ball, David!" a voice shouts when I return to the beach the next morning.

"Throw it again, Daddy!" a child shouts back.

The beach is empty except for the father and son. I feel a wave of sadness when I look at them. They look so happy. I wonder if my parents were ever that happy playing with me.

The breeze whips up, stinging my eyes. I wipe away tears, pretending I'm crying because of the wind. I haven't heard from my parents in two days.

Mobile reception is spotty here. I have to walk into town to get a signal. Even then it only works half the time. The last time we talked, my parents told me they were trying couples therapy. I'm glad neither of my parents has moved out yet.

"Back here, David!" the man calls again.

The boy is about four years old. He scoops up a neon pink ball and hurls it towards his dad. The ball flies over his dad's head and into the waves. The dad is laughing as he runs to get it. Another man walks down the sand dunes towards the boy.

"Daddy!" the boy yells, running to the other man. The first man jogs up to them and they all hug. A perfect, happy family. So different from mine.

My parents have always had a rocky relationship. Mum married Dad two days after graduating from university. They had planned on travelling the world, but my mum's dad got sick. They stayed in Birmingham to take care of him. After he died, my dad started studying for his Master's degree, and my mum had a job. Then I was born. Mum named me India, because it was the country she most wanted to visit.

I told them they should spend the summer travelling, but Mum said they couldn't afford it.

"I'm not sure it would solve our problems anyway, sweet pea," she said, brushing my hair off my forehead.

Instead they sent me to Cornwall. I wonder what my life will be like when I return.

The family has left the beach. Sand stretches on either side of me until the beach runs into low cliffs. I could be the only person in the world.

The thought scares me.

"Why won't you call me?" I ask the waves, looking up and down the shore for a wreath.

I spend the next half hour walking every millimetre of shoreline. I don't see a single piece of seaweed, much less an entire wreath.

I plop back down onto the sand.

"This is silly," I say. I feel as if I'm the girl waiting for the boy to call her. I've never wanted to be that girl.

I jump to my feet and head towards the cliffs. "If you won't talk to me, I'll talk to you," I mutter.

I climb over the smooth rocks to where the forest begins. Thick pine trees cover the cliffs. The ground is soft and spongy beneath my feet. Wild flower season is over. Maybe I'll find some branches that will work.

The day I arrived in Cornwall, Grandpa took me to the shore and tossed a wreath of wild flowers into the water. I wasn't sure what he was doing. Later, when he told me about the mermaids, he explained that he sent the wreath to tell them I was here.

"Another Finch has arrived to help," Grandpa said.

"And another Finch is still here," I say beneath the pine trees. Soon I've gathered an armful of branches. I head back to the beach and sit on the sand.

As I weave my wreath, I think about the time I first discovered my mer powers. It was my second time in the water and my first visit to the mer. My first time in the water, I had just met my mermaid friends, Lulu, Dana and Nari. Grandpa had been telling me about my mermaid heritage. I didn't believe him, so he brought me to the cliffs and pushed me into the water. My mermaid friends found me and started teaching me about mer life.

A few days later, my friends called for me by sending a wreath. I was nervous as I hovered over the water, Grandpa at my side.

"Take a deep breath, India," he said.

"Do I need to hold my breath when I jump in?" I asked. I was worried I'd forgotten how to activate my mer abilities.

"Your body knows what to do when it gets into the ocean," Grandpa said. "I told you to breathe because you look as if you are going to be sick."

"Oh," I said. I took a deep breath and felt better. I swung my arms the way I do before a big swimming race. My nerves calmed down.

"You'll be fine," Grandpa said. "Go now."

I took one last look at his face. His eyes looked sad.

"Are you okay, Grandpa?" I asked.

He placed a hand on my shoulder. "I'm fine, India." His hand dropped. "I'm proud of you. But you have a lot of responsibility ahead of you."

I wasn't sure what to say. "I haven't done anything yet," I said.

"You're carrying on our legacy," he said. "You're returning to our mer family."

"Um, okay," I said.

That was one of the first times Grandpa talked about the mer as family. I was just excited to swim with dolphins and see where my mermaid friends lived. But I also felt some relief. Sometimes my family seemed so small. And it would get even smaller if Mum and Dad split up. With the mer, I had a place. I belonged. At least I hoped so.

"Be safe, India," Grandpa said.

I looked at the waves crashing beneath my feet. "See you soon, Grandpa," I said.

Then I jumped.

My friends were waiting for me at the base of the cliff. Lulu, with her skin darker than mine and her bright green tail. Dana with her pale face and thick red hair, her pink tail flapping. Nari with her sweet smile, dark eyes and blue tail.

"You made it," Lulu said.

"Welcome back," Nari said, giving me a hug.

I grinned, relieved that I was easily breathing water.

"Hi, everybody," I said.

"Ready?" Dana asked, a glint in her eye.

"For what?" I asked. But we were already off, bolting through the water like bullets. The morning was beautiful. The water was clear, and the sun shone above us. We played with dolphins and chased silvery fish. We didn't see any sharks or giant squid – the only animals who hurt the mer. I ate seaweed for the first time, and I didn't hate it. It reminded me of the vegetarian sushi we used to have on Friday nights at home.

We were supposed to go to Ice Canyon so I could meet Ani, Lulu's mother and the leader of the Ice Canyon tribe. We'd stopped near a pile of rocks for lunch. My friends were showing me their powers. Dana made the water thick, like jelly. Lulu changed the currents so the jelly water floated like a beach ball. Nari summoned two dolphins to play with the ball.

"Jump in any time, India," Lulu called, teasing me. We were hoping that seeing their powers would activate mine.

"Maybe my power is telling jokes," I said.

"Not likely," Dana said, giggling.

I tossed a handful of seaweed at her. She moved to avoid it and crashed into Lulu. Dana somehow tripped over Lulu's tail, and her hands smashed into the rocks.

"Oh, no!" Nari gasped as Dana's blood pooled in the water.

"It's fine, just a scratch," Dana said. I was already swimming towards her, my palms itching.

"Here," I said, grabbing her hands.

Dana was too surprised to protest. I cupped her hands in mine. Thin scratches crossed her palms, still bleeding.

I knew exactly what to do. I closed my eyes and felt waves of power flow through me. I covered Dana's cuts with my hand. When I removed my hand, her cuts were gone.

"That's amazing," Nari breathed, looking over Dana's shoulder.

"Wow," I said. I had no idea I could do anything like that. I enjoyed the first-aid courses at school, but I'd never done anything like this on land.

"Well, I guess we know what your powers are," Lulu said. Even she looked impressed.

"There aren't many mermaids who have healing powers," Dana explained. "It's really rare. Usually only one or two mermaids in a generation."

"Really?" I asked.

"I guess this means you'll get to visit a lot," Lulu said. "Your powers will be really helpful to the mer."

Not helpful enough, I think, returning to the present. A rough wreath lies in my lap. I get to my feet and walk to the edge of the water. The tide is going out.

"If you thought my gifts were so important, why don't you call for me more?" I ask.

I take the wreath in both hands and fling it as hard as I can. It bobs on the water. I watch as it slips beyond the waves, heading further out to sea. I watch it until I can't see it anymore. I look for a fin or a head poking up through the water.

Nothing.

I wait on the shore for hours. Finally, as the beach fills with happy families behind me, I go home alone.

CHAPTER 3

Two days later, there's still no sign of a wreath from my friends.

"Where the heck are you guys?" I say, scowling at the waves.

I check my phone. In an hour, I'm supposed to be at the museum to sort more fish hooks.

I think about the piles of twisted metal that await me. And I make a decision.

"If you won't come to me, I'll just have to go to you," I say.

I run back to the cottage and leave a note for Grandpa. I'm starving, so I open the kitchen cupboards. A few dusty cereal bars lurk in a corner.

Gross, I think. I guess I'll just make do with the seaweed. It's not very tasty, but I can't bring any human food into the ocean. It would get wet. Anyway, I lose my appetite for human food when I'm in the water.

A few minutes later I'm climbing over jagged rocks. Waves crash beneath my feet. The wind has picked up, and I'm almost blown over. I take one last look at the empty beach to make sure no one sees, then I dive into the waves.

I feel lost, like I always do when I first jump into the ocean. My lungs take a few moments to adjust to breathing water instead of air. I feel as if I'm going to choke. I hate that feeling.

My hands go to my throat. I cough, and then suddenly my lungs open up. I start breathing water.

I open my eyes, flinching as the salt water stings them. I float in the waves for a few minutes until my eyes are better.

A big wave comes up and pushes me close to the cliffs. Shards of brightly coloured plastic swirl around me. Human pollution. I bat the plastic away from my head. Then I find the rocks with my bare feet and push off.

Soon I'm free of the tides and the rocks. I'm breathing water easily now, and my eyes no longer sting. I love how I can see beneath the waves. If humans get too deep, the water gets dark. For me, it's different. Everything is bright during the day. I can see for miles.

I find myself laughing as I slice through the water. I feel free and alive.

As I move into open water, I'm met with a surprise.

"Evan," I say. I stare at the merman floating in front of me.

I've had a crush on Evan ever since I first met him. He's cute, with light brown skin and dark brown hair. His tail is dark green, like a forest at night. I like his eyes the best, the way they look deeply at me. Right now they are looking at me with surprise.

"India?" he asks, swimming closer.

"Hi, Evan," I say, giving a weak wave.

"What are you doing out here?" he asks. "They didn't summon you."

"How do you know that?" I ask.

Evan blushes, which is adorable. "I ... um ... I asked Dana to tell me when they were summoning you," he confesses.

I'm sure my grin could light up the ocean. "You did?" I ask. My voice squeaks.

"Yeah," he says.

"Why?" I ask. The word slips out before I can stop it.

Evan shrugs his shoulders. "I didn't want to miss you," he says. "I know you're going back to Birmingham at the end of the summer. I wanted to make sure I saw you before you went."

His words make me feel as if there's a balloon inside me getting bigger and bigger. I'm so happy I could explode. "Well, I'm not going back yet. There's still a lot of summer to go," I say.

"I'm glad," Evan says, swimming closer to me.

"Me too," I say. A thought occurs to me. "So what are you doing out here? You're a long way from the canyons."

If possible, Evan blushes an even darker red. "Um, well, don't get freaked out. But sometimes I come out here to see you," he says.

"Why would that freak me out?" I ask. I can't help feeling excited that he looks for me sometimes.

"I'm not stalking you or anything," he says. "I just ... missed you."

"Me too," I say simply. We start swimming away from shore. "Do you ever see me?"

"Sometimes," Evan says. "A few days ago I saw you walking along the shore. I thought maybe you were looking for a wreath."

"I was," I admit. "A wreath that never came." I hope that when Evan saw me, I wasn't doing something silly like scratching my butt.

"They still haven't sent you a wreath," he says.

"Right," I say.

"So why are you out here?" he asks. "Did someone else summon you?"

I stop swimming, kicking my legs to tread water. "No one summoned me," I say. "I came out here on my own."

"You're trying to get to the canyons on your own?" Evan asks, looking a little bit shocked. "But I didn't think you could find them without a mer guide."

"I can't," I confess, feeling embarrassed. "But I missed my friends. I missed hanging out at the canyons and visiting the *Clemmons* and ... and everything."

I'm not sure why I can't quite come out and say I missed Evan. But he seems to know that I did.

"Everything?" he asks with a grin.

"Fine, I missed you too," I say, returning the smile. "It's been a while since I visited."

"Does your grandpa know you're here?" Evan asks.

"I left him a note. Does that count?" I ask.

Evan looks confused. I remember that the mer don't have a written language.

"I left him a sign that I was leaving," I correct.

"Will he be okay with it?" Evan asks.

"Probably not," I say. "But neither will the mer if I get to the canyons."

I keep treading water, moving neither forwards nor backwards. "Maybe this wasn't such a good idea," I say. "Maybe I should go back."

Evan catches my hand. "Don't," he says. "If you want to see your friends that badly, you should. I'll take you to the canyons."

"You will?" I ask. My voice sounds squeaky again.

"Sure," he says. He holds out his hand. "Shall we?"

CHAPTER 4

It's not easy swimming while holding someone's hand. Eventually Evan and I are forced to let go, but I can feel his fingers around mine the rest of the trip. The day is beautiful. Along the way, Evan tells me the latest news.

"My dad and Ani held another all-tribe dinner two nights ago," he says.

"How did that go?" I ask.

Storm, Evan's father, is the leader of the Fire Canyon tribe.

The Fire and Ice Canyon tribes do not get along well. Mainly because the Fire Canyon tribe wants to wipe humans off the face of the earth. The Ice Canyon tribe is content to leave humans alone.

Ani and Storm want to improve relationships between the tribes. The dinners are a way to bring the mer together.

"It went okay," Evan says. "Only two fights, and neither drew blood."

"I guess that's good," I say. "How does your dad think it's going?" I'm never excited to see Storm. He doesn't like me much. Not surprising, considering his tribe hates humans.

"He doesn't talk about it much," Evan says. "Melody thinks Storm should talk to me about it more. If he's grooming me to take over as leader someday."

"Melody?" I ask, coming to a stop.

Evan looks confused. "Well, yeah. You know Melody, right?"

"Of course I know Melody," I say. My mind flashes to the mermaid with the golden hair and blue eyes. "I didn't think you hung out with her much."

Evan chews his lip, deep in thought. "I don't know. I guess we do," he says after a while. "Wait, is that a problem?"

My heart feels lighter. Evan seemed confused that I was jealous. I hope that means there's nothing going on with him and Melody. Then my heart falls. Maybe it means there's nothing going on with Evan and me.

Evan swims closer to me and reaches out. He doesn't seem sure where to touch me. In the end, his fingers brush the edge of my elbow.

"I like you, India Finch," he says. "I can stop hanging out with Melody if it bothers you."

I let out a breath of water. "You should hang out with whoever you want," I say. "And ... and I like you too."

Evan beams and blushes at the same time. He brushes my elbow one more time. "Should we get going?" he asks.

"Lead on," I say.

Soon we are at Ice Canyon.

"What does the dome look like today?" I ask. I can't see or feel the dome, even though I know it's there, protecting the mer.

"Blue," he says.

"Bright blue or dark blue?" I ask.

Evan pauses, looking over my head at the invisible dome. "The kind of blue the sky gets right before the sun rises," he says.

"That's pretty language for a Fire Canyon kid," a voice rasps behind us.

We whirl round to see a group of three guards floating behind us. Two mermen and a mermaid. Their eyes flicker over me.

"You were not summoned, India Finch," the mermaid says. Her red hair is pulled back tightly.

"H-h-how do you ... how do you know that?" I stammer.

The guards look at each other. "Because we are told when you are summoned," one of the mermen says, his purple tail swishing. "And we were not told this time."

“We are always told,” the third one repeats. His eyes narrow. “And your Fire Canyon friend is not welcome here.”

I stiffen, anger racing through me. “Why not?” I challenge. “He has just as much a right to be here as I do.”

The guards laugh, a sharp, brittle sound. “That’s true,” the mermaid says. Her red ponytail floats in the water behind her. “Neither of you have any right to be here.”

Their hands tighten on the harpoons they carry. The long spears are topped with sharp tips. A nasty thought jumps into my mind. *They wouldn’t have any problem using the harpoons on me.*

My dad has taught me how to deal with angry people in power. I slow my breathing. I unclench my hands. And I make my voice pleasant.

“We didn’t mean to cause trouble,” I say. “We’re sorry for bothering you. We’ll leave you alone now.”

Evan is staring at me. I take his arm and gently tug him backwards.

"Not so fast," the second guard says, lifting his harpoon. "You need to come with us."

The other two move to surround us. I grab Evan's hand. "Where are you taking us?" I ask.

"Why? Are you afraid, little girl?" one sneers.

"You're not wanted here," another says.

"We'll take you somewhere far from here," the third says.

"Hold on," Evan says. "You're not going to do anything to her."

"Oh, you're invited too," the first one says. "Since you are so fond of humans, you deserve their fate."

"Traitor," the mermaid guard spits.

"Come with us," the first one says again.

I'm terrified. No one knows we're here. If they take us somewhere, no one would even be looking for us.

"Please, we don't mean any harm," I say. My words are tight with fear, even though I'm trying to stay calm. "There's no need to–"

"What seems to be the problem?" a new voice interrupts.

My knees go weak when I realize it's Bruce, the one guard who likes me. His grey hair is cut close to his head. His sharp nose makes him look like a hawk. He beats the water with his silver tail.

The other guards glare at Bruce.

"They're not supposed to be here," the mermaid says. She points at me. "She was not summoned." Then she points at Evan. "Neither was he."

Bruce runs a hand through his hair. "Is that so?" he asks.

The mermaid glares at him. "Yes, it's so!" she yells. "We just told you."

"That's true, that's true," Bruce murmurs. He glances overhead, and I wonder if he's looking at the dome. "Still not much of a problem, though," he continues, "seeing as they're my guests."

The other guards look angry and surprised.

"They're your guests?" the second guard says doubtfully. He crosses his arms over his wide belly.

"Yep," Bruce says.

"And I suppose you summoned them?" the mermaid challenges.

"Nope," Bruce answers. "But you never know when you're going to run into friends." He swims towards Evan and me and throws an arm over our shoulders. "Good to see you, India. I can't thank you enough for healing my cut last time you were here."

"No problem," I say, my voice shaking.

"And, Evan, glad you're back," Bruce adds. "I'm sure Storm would be happy his son is doing the same work as his father. Trying to bring the tribes together."

"Thank you, sir," Evan says.

Bruce laughs. "No need to call me sir," he says. "Now, let's see about getting you some food. You must be tired after your journey."

We don't look back to see if the guards are watching us. I know they must be, because I can feel their eyes shooting daggers into my back.

When we get to the first towering rock wall, Bruce lets us go.

"That was a close one," he says. "I don't mind either of you being here, but you have to be more careful."

"Thanks, Bruce," I say.

"Yeah, thanks," Evan adds.

Bruce gazes at us for a long moment. I realize his eyes are as hawk-like as his nose. "Stay out of trouble, you two." He looks gruff, but he's smiling a little.

"See you around, Bruce," I say.

He gives a wave as he swims away.

I turn to face Evan, who is looking as shaken as I feel. "That was close," I say. "And it's my fault."

"Not your fault," Evan says.

"Yes it is," I say. "I'm the one who insisted on coming here. No one called for me. I just came. And I'm starting to see why that's a bad idea."

Evan catches my hand. "I'm still glad you're here."

His head dips forwards. For a second I think he is going to kiss me. I'll never know, though, because at that moment, my friends arrive.

"India!" they shriek.

A mass of arms and tails descends on me. I can't even tell who is hugging me. When we finally separate, my three friends are grinning at me.

Lulu, Dana and Nari. And me. We're finally together. Suddenly everything seems right.

"Let's go to the *Clemmons*," I say, picturing the sunk steamer ship where the younger mer hang out.

"Uh-oh," Lulu says, glancing over my shoulder.

"I think we'll have to postpone that trip," Nari whispers, squeezing my hand.

"I don't think I've ever seen Ani look that angry," Dana says.

Only then do I turn around. Ani is swimming towards me, her face stony with anger.

"India Finch," she says when she gets to us. "You've got some explaining to do. All of you. To my cave. *Now*!"

CHAPTER 5

Ani yells at me for hours. At least it seems that way. She goes through all of the reasons why it was a bad idea for me to come here without being summoned.

"You could have been hurt on the trip and no one would know!" she says at one point. I don't bother mentioning that Evan was with me the whole time. I don't think she wants to hear any reply from me.

Out of the corner of my eye, I see my friends pressed up against the wall. Their eyes are glued to Ani.

"And the guards!" Ani says, flinging up her hands. "They didn't know ahead of time to let you in! At least my guards recognized you so you weren't in danger."

"But we *were* in danger," I say. "The guards we met threatened us." I look to Evan for backup. He's floating near the entrance of the cave, looking as if he wants to be anywhere else.

"What?" Ani asks, looking confused.

"It's true," Evan says. "They had harpoons. Things would have gotten bad if the other guard hadn't shown up."

"Bruce," I add. "He's the one who helped us. He talked down the other guards and got us away from them."

Ani's face is grim. She swims towards me. "Are you telling me that my guards made you feel unsafe?"

"Yes," I say. "They were going to take us away. I think they were going to hurt us."

Ani's face collapses, and she instantly drags me into her arms.

"My poor girl," she says, smoothing my brown curls. She looks over to Evan. "And my poor boy. That's no way to treat our guests. I didn't know. I will deal with them."

"Okay," I say. No one's hugged me like this since I last saw my mum.

Ani lets me go. "I'm still angry with you," she says, although her voice is soft and kind now.

"I know," I say. I ask the question I've been dreading: "Are you going to send me home?"

Ani brushes another curl away from my face. "I should. Does your grandfather know you're here?"

"Yes," I say. I decide Ani doesn't need to know that I only left him a note before running off.

"I will send someone to tell him you made it here safely," she says. "You went through all of this trouble to get here. I suppose you can stay for a few days. The jellyfish have been bad this year. You could heal some jellyfish stings."

"Hooray!" my friends yell, exploding from the wall.

"But only a few days," Ani says. "And we will put you to work. After that, we're sending you back."

I give her another hug and then race with my friends out of the cave.

Freedom tastes wonderful. Like Cornish pasties and ice cream cones and cotton candy. Freedom is beautiful too. The water looks brighter, and the anemones dotting the canyon walls shimmer. A school of tuna swims through the canyon, and I have the urge to chase them. I feel as if I'd be happy for the rest of my life if I lived here.

"What should we do first?" I ask.

"Do?" Lulu asks.

"Yeah, let's go and do something!" I say.

Dana looks at me as if I've grown two heads. "I guess we could go to the *Clemmons*."

"That sounds great!" I say. "Let's do whatever you do on a normal day."

My friends give me weird looks.

"What?" I ask.

Nari is the first to answer. "We don't really *do* a lot," she says.

"What do you mean?" I ask. "What do you usually do when I'm not here?"

My friends exchange looks. "Well, we swim sometimes," Dana says.

"And sometimes we talk to the other mer at the *Clemmons,*" Lulu says.

"There was that one time we gathered seaweed for dinner," Nari says. "But that was at least a year ago."

I glance at Evan. He doesn't look concerned. "What do you usually do?" I ask him.

"The same," he says. "Sometimes we play our rock game. There's usually a game at the *Clemmons*."

"Great, let's do that!" I say. I charge ahead, barely noticing that my friends are lagging behind.

In a few minutes, we're at the *Clemmons*. The ship sits lopsided on the sandy ocean floor. When it sank, it landed on one side. I've always thought it looks like something from a movie. Most of the hull has peeled away, revealing a twisted maze of hallways.

"Let's see who can swim through to the other side first!" I shout, charging ahead. I'm deep in the belly of the ship before I realize I'm alone.

When I poke my head back out, my friends are floating near the deck. A few other mer float nearby.

"Where did you guys go?" I ask, swimming up to them.

Dana toys with the end of her red hair. "Oh, sorry," she said, dropping her braid. "We thought we'd get the news from the other mer first."

I glance at the other mer, who aren't saying anything. "Okay, so what do they know?" I ask.

A young mer with an orange tail looks over at me. "Nothing much," he says.

"We don't know much, either," Nari says.

Then they keep floating there. And floating. Not saying a thing.

"Um, guys?" I finally interrupt. Every head turns to look at me. "Is there more to talk about? Or can we go and do something now?"

Lulu looks at me, puzzled. "We are doing something, India," she explains.

"You're just floating here," I say.

Every mer on deck looks confused.

"This is a normal day for us," the mer with the orange tail says. "We will be tired tonight."

"Oh, okay," I say, thinking fast. "Um, Nari? Can I talk to you?"

"Sure," she says, her sapphire tail glinting in the water. We swim a short distance away.

"What's up?" Nari asks.

"Are you kidding me?" I ask. "This is what's up." I point at the silent group of floating mer. "No one's talking. No one's doing anything. And that guy said this is really tiring for you. What's happening?"

It takes Nari a few moments to work out what I'm asking. "Is this not what you do on land?" she asks.

I think of my friends back home in Birmingham. We have a spot by the river where we hang out until our curfews. We talk and throw Frisbees and sometimes have a game of football. I suppose anyone watching us would think we're not doing much. But we're certainly doing more than the mer.

"Usually when we hang out, we're still doing something," I say. "Even if it's just talking. We're at least, you know, talking. To each other."

Nari tilts her head to one side, her dark hair falling in a curtain over her shoulder. "Oh," she says. "No wonder you keep asking us to do something. You're bored."

She's right. I am bored. I hate to admit it, because I love the mer. But if this is all they do, I might as well go home.

"I don't get it," I say. "Other times I've been here, we've done a ton of stuff. We're always busy."

Nari laughs, a sound like bells. "Every other time you've been here, we had a task. We had to heal something or save something. There was a purpose." She waves in the direction of the mer. "When there's not a problem to solve, this is what mer life looks like."

My heart sinks as I look at the deck of the *Clemmons*. No one has moved. No one is talking. Not even Evan. I'm struck by a horrible realization – are my friends boring?

Nari links her arm through mine. "What would you like to do?" she asks.

"Well, we could go for a swim," I suggest. "Talk maybe. Or explore something. Like check out more of the *Clemmons*."

Nari chews her bottom lip, nodding. "You're right. That does sound fun." She turns to the larger group. "Hey, everyone," Nari calls. "India's right. We should do something!"

CHAPTER 6

Half an hour later, we are doing something – just not what I expected. I thought we'd swim to the edge of the dome. Or maybe have a race or something. Or share a conversation where we actually talked.

Instead the mer have discovered a new game – showing off our powers. Only the mermaids can play, since the boys don't have powers.

The game was Evan's idea. I had suggested exploring the ship, but one of the Ice Canyon mermaids, Shana, said a door had collapsed on the far side. A rock had fallen on it. We'd have to move the rock before we could explore, since the doorway was the only way out on the other side.

Fortunately, Shana's power is moving heavy objects. We all followed her around to the side of the ship to watch. The rock crushing the doors was taller than me. We watched as Shana picked up the rock as easily as if it were a tiny sea urchin.

"That was so cool," Evan said. He turned to me. "You all have amazing powers. I wish I could see more of them."

"You've already seen my powers," a voice interrupted. "Lots of times." Melody swam up to us, her blond hair cascading through the currents.

I don't like Melody very much. She doesn't like me, either. We've never hit it off. Both of us liking Evan probably has something to do with it.

"That's true," Evan said, blushing.

"I don't think I've ever seen your powers, Melody," I said. "I didn't even think you had any."

Melody's eyes narrowed at me. "Maybe you haven't been paying attention," she said, looping an arm across Evan's shoulders. To my relief, he shook it free.

"Hey, maybe all of the mermaids should have a contest," Evan suggested. "Show off their powers."

Everyone loved this idea. So here we are, showing off our powers for the boys.

"My mum would hate this," I say as Shana lifts a rock the size of a car. Lulu and I are in the back near the *Clemmons*.

"Why?" Lulu asks.

"You've got all of the mermaids competing while the boys judge us," I say. "She hates stuff like that."

"But why?" Lulu presses.

"Because men are always judging women," I grumble.

"But down here, mermaids are stronger than mermen," Lulu says. "We have powers. They don't."

"Oh," I say. I hadn't thought about it like that. It's another reminder that the world under the ocean is different from the world I live in. "Do the mermen ever think it's unfair?"

Lulu shakes her head. "We all work together. The mermen gather our food. We keep everyone safe. It's just the way things are."

"Look." Dana nudges me with her elbow.

Melody is taking her turn, swimming in front of the crowd with a saucy flip of her ice blue tail. I don't know what to expect. No one has told me what Melody's powers are.

I know as soon as she opens her mouth.

I like all kinds of music: R & B, soul, rock, hip-hop. I don't even mind when my mum blasts Neil Diamond through the house. But what Melody does is more than music. Better than music. She opens her mouth, and magic pours out.

Soon everyone is swaying in a daze. Evan looks half in love. Heck, *I* feel half in love with Melody when she sings. I finally understand all of those stories about the Sirens, the mermaids who lured sailors to their deaths.

I lose track of how long Melody sings. I forget who I am and what I'm doing here. All I want is to be close to that voice.

"Hey, you okay?" Lulu asks, shaking my elbow.

I jump. "What's happening?" I ask.

Lulu squints at me. "How much do you remember?"

"Huh?" I ask.

"Of what just happened?" she asks, gesturing towards Melody.

Memories are hazy. "Um, Melody was singing?" I ask.

"Yes," Lulu says. "Anything else?"

"Not really. Why? Did I do something dumb?" I ask.

"You stared at her for a while," Lulu says.

"Oh, well, didn't you?" I ask, my face heating up.

"Melody has a beautiful voice, but it didn't make me forget myself," Lulu says. She looks me over. "Must be your half-human side."

"I don't know how we're going to top that," Dana grumbles.

"That was beautiful," Nari gushes as Melody swims past us.

"Thanks," she says. She glances at me. "And what did you think, India?"

I decide to take the high road. "Your voice is wonderful," I say.

Melody frowns for a moment. She's probably trying to decide if I'm making fun of her or not.

"Well, Evan certainly thinks so," she finally says. She flips her hair and swims over to Evan.

"You're up," the mer with the orange tail calls to us. I really should learn that guy's name. Too late. My friends are already dragging me in front of the mer.

"What should we do?" I whisper. "Am I supposed to cut one of you and then heal it? I don't want to do that."

"No, I have an idea," Lulu says to us. "People of the mer, listen to me!" She raises her voice to address the crowd.

"She looks just like Ani," Dana whispers.

"Sounds like her too," Nari says.

Lulu doesn't hear us. "Mermaid powers are impressive on their own," she says to the crowd. "But they are even stronger together."

She motions us to gather at her side.

"What are we going to do?" Dana asks.

"Follow my lead," Lulu says.

Beating her tail hard, Lulu raises her arms and summons a current. Water starts flowing past us. I almost get swept off my feet but Nari catches my arm at the last minute.

"What does she want us to do?" Nari whispers.

"I'm not sure," I say, watching as Lulu's wave gets stronger and stronger.

Dana catches on first. She swims to Lulu's side and raises her own hands. Soon the texture of the water changes. In a minute, the wave is thick like jelly. The water looks like a tornado now, spinning slowly in place like a giant top.

"Oh, I see," Nari says. She breaks away from me and swims to the others.

"Wait, what do you see?" I'm calling after her but she doesn't answer.

"Watch!" Nari says. She gets a distant look in her eyes, and I realize she's calling to animals with her mind. Soon a school of silvery fish surround Nari. She nods, and they leap into the spinning water.

If the water was spinning fast, it would be cruel. But Lulu's water tornado is turning about as fast as the world's slowest merry-go-round. The fish are fine. In fact, this would be a great activity for a kids' birthday party.

I like seeing my friends work together. All of the mer are amazed by the trick. Lulu wiggles her fingers, and the tornado starts to expand ever so slowly. Soon the mer who are watching back up.

Lulu looks over at me and cocks her head. "India! Come play with us!"

I swim forwards, all eyes on me. Evan gives me a thumbs-up as I pass. Melody scowls, but I ignore her.

When I reach my friends, I'm not sure what to do. The tornado is even bigger up close. I reach my hand forwards and let my fingers trail in the thick water.

"This is really cool!" I say.

"Play with us," Lulu repeats.

"How?" I ask. "It doesn't need to be healed." As soon as I say the words, an idea occurs to me. I stretch both of my hands forwards this time.

I take a breath. I hold it. Then I touch the tornado with my healing power.

BAM! There is a sizzle and a flash of lightning. A huge explosion knocks us back. I can see mer flailing in the water, their mouths open. They must be shouting, but all I hear is silence.

What's happening? Why can't I hear anything? I think.

I press my hands to my ears. I can't even hear the sound of water.

Lulu grabs my arm. Her mouth moves too, but I have no idea what she's saying. I point to my ears. My hands fall to my side as I look over Lulu's shoulder.

The tornado has turned into a wave. A giant, horrible, epic tidal wave. The water is as thick as pudding and moving as fast as a bullet.

And it's heading towards land. When it hits, it will be like a train slamming into a building at full speed.

"Oh, no," I breathe.

Sounds start coming back to me, muffled. I feel as if someone taped cotton wool over my ears.

"–won't be able to get away in time!" Lulu is shouting.

"–have to go before–" Dana says.

"India? India!" Nari yells, shaking my arm.

"Can't hear well," I say. My voice sounds as if I'm talking from the bottom of a well.

Lulu nods. "The wave," she says, speaking loudly. "It's going to hit land. We have to stop it."

"Never going to work," someone mumbles. After a moment I realize I'm the one who spoke.

Evan blazes up to us. "India!" he shouts, wrapping an arm around me. "Are you okay?"

"No. Not okay," I say, shaking my head. "My ears."

Evan starts to speak, but I shake my head. I can't hear him. He puts his mouth against my ear.

"Heal," he says. His lips are warm against my skin.

I shake my head. I don't trust my powers right now, not after what just happened with the wave.

Evan won't let me give up. He stops and takes both of my hands in his, planting them over my ears. "Do it," he says.

He's saying more, but I can't hear him. He's right, though. I have to heal myself. If I don't, I won't be any good at stopping the wave.

I take a breath and channel powers into my ears. In a moment, the cotton clears.

Screams fill my ears. For a moment, I wish I hadn't healed myself. The sounds are terrible. I'd do anything to make them go away.

The wave is picking up speed as it races away. I can see tiny silver fish whirling in terror.

"Those poor fish," Nari says, sounding heartbroken.

"Come on!" Lulu shouts.

We all race to catch up with her. Evan is at my side, his hand around my elbow. We swim awkwardly, but I'm glad he's next to me.

"Stop it!" someone shouts. Most of the mer from the *Clemmons* are swimming with us. Everyone's faces are wide with terror.

The wave has picked up even more speed. My friends have caught up with it. Lulu and Dana are waving their hands as they try to swim. Nari is shouting at the tiny fish in the thick water.

"We have to stop it!" another voice adds.

They're right. If the massive wave hits land, it will cause major damage. Scientists will wonder where the wave came from. If they look hard enough, they might find the mer. And it will be my fault.

"Evan!" I shout, grabbing his hands. "You have to help me."

Evan's face looks grim. "You don't have much time left," he says. He points in the direction of the wave. I can't believe it's possible, but the wave is even bigger. Lulu and Dana have fallen behind. Nari is no longer yelling at the wave. Instead she's swimming alongside it. I'm not sure what she's doing.

"Let's go," I say, grabbing Evan's hand.

I'm a fast swimmer, but Evan is even faster. I kick my legs faster than I ever have before, trying to keep up with him.

Soon we're near the wave. It has stopped growing, but it is still racing towards land.

"What's Nari doing?" I ask as we catch up to Lulu and Dana. Lulu's face is grey.

"She's trying to warn sea creatures to stay out of the way. She gave up on helping the ones in the wave. They're stuck."

"Because of us," Dana whispers. She looks so pale that I think she might faint.

"No, because of me," I say. "I'm the one who gave it a burst of power."

"There's no time for blame," Evan says. "Come on."

With his free hand, Evan takes Lulu's hand and starts swimming. Lulu grabs Dana and the four of us race after the wave.

"Start fixing it!" Evan calls over the roar of water.

Dana raises her free hand and tries to make the water thinner. Lulu drops Evan's hand and starts swirling the currents again. I don't know what I can do. If I try to heal the wave, it might only make it bigger.

And then it looks as if we've won. Lulu's new currents are shifting the wave into a slightly different path. Dana has made the water thinner. A few of the silvery fish have even escaped.

I start to relax. We'll send the wave out to sea. Eventually it will die down. No one will get hurt. We won't even need to tell Ani what happened. Everything will be fine.

I start to tell this to Evan, but his hand tightens on mine. His face is tilted towards the surface. His mouth opens in horror.

I follow his gaze.

"Oh, no," I whisper.

A small ship bobs on the surface of the water. And the wave is heading right towards it.

CHAPTER 7

The boat floats overhead, looking flimsy and fragile. I can't do anything but watch as the giant wave we created slams into it.

The ship breaks apart like a child's Lego set. The ocean churns. People start falling into the water. Their legs and arms kick, toothpicks fighting against the English Channel.

"We have to help them," I say. I shoot towards the surface, dragging Evan with me.

"India, what are you doing?" Lulu shouts. She blocks us before we reach the shipwreck.

I push past her. "Get out of my way, Lulu," I say.

Lulu grabs my wrist. "India, stop."

"No!" I shout. "I'm not going to let those people die."

Lulu's face looks sad and angry. "We can't risk being seen. Don't you get it?" she cries.

I stare at my friends. Dana and Nari are floating behind Lulu. I glance at Evan, whose face is blank.

"You can't be serious," I say to them. "You're not going to help?"

Nari glances at the surface, looking worried. She might be my only hope. I know how sensitive she is.

"Think of the people up there, Nari. People who look like me," I say.

Nari chews her lip, but she doesn't say anything. Evan's hand shifts in mine. Dana and Lulu look uncomfortable.

"There are families up there," I say, addressing all of them. "Parents and children. Grandparents. And we're just going to let them die?" My voice cracks on the last words.

Dana breaks the silence. "What if they see us?" she asks.

"Who cares?" I say. The words spit out of my mouth. "Lives are at stake. They are living creatures. Just like you. And they don't want to drown in the ocean."

I risk a glance overhead. People are still flailing in the water. They will tire quickly in the cold water.

"We did this," I say. "All of us. We made the wave. Now we need to take responsibility."

Evan's fingers tighten around mine. "She's right," he says right before he zooms towards the surface.

"Well?" I ask the rest of them. "I'm going with Evan. What are you going to do?"

I'm almost out of time, but my friends aren't moving. "Fine," I say. I follow Evan to the shipwreck, leaving my friends behind. As I swim, I wipe tears from my eyes.

I break the surface of the water. My lungs gasp as I start breathing air. I cough, hating the extra moments keeping me from helping.

The shipwreck is a mess. Bits of the hull float on the water. There are pieces of plastic and wood littering the surface. Up close, I can hear screams.

"My babies! Where are my babies?" one woman shrieks. Another man shouts the name *Max* over and over again.

My heart breaks, and I'm furious with myself. Why did I waste all of that time arguing with my friends?

"India! Over here!" Evan's voice calls over the noise.

I race in his direction. Along the way I notice something troubling. I don't see a single lifeboat.

"Help me!" Evan says. He's clinging to a piece of the ship. His arms strain as he tries to flip the piece over. No wonder. The piece is the size of a minivan.

"What are you trying to do?" I ask as I reach him.

"Lifeboats," he gasps. "Trapped."

Understanding dawns on me. I take a breath and dive beneath the water. A tangle of lifeboats floats upside down beneath the wreckage.

"We have to flip it," I say, resurfacing.

"I can't do it alone," Evan says, still straining.

I place my hands on the piece of the ship and lift with all of my might. My hands slip, and my muscles feel as if they're going to tear. The piece is too heavy. We can't move it.

"If we don't get these people into lifeboats, they'll die," I shout over the churning water.

Evan grits his jaw and keeps pushing at the piece. "I can't get enough of a grip," he says.

Around us, the screams are getting quieter.

"It's going to be too late," I say. Pain and anger rip through me. "They're going to die."

Evan takes my hand. "We can't give up," he says.

He's right. I stay at his side, trying to flip the wreckage. My legs kick wildly to stay afloat. I'm not sure how much longer I can do this.

Suddenly we're not alone.

"Stand back," Lulu says. She floats a few metres behind us.

"Lulu?" I gape.

"Move," she says. She catches my eye. "It will be all right, India."

Evan and I move to the side. Dana and Nari join us. "What's she going to do?" I whisper to Dana.

"You'll see," she says, her face tight with worry.

Lulu raises her hand. A surge of water moves around us. A mini wave appears, a small cousin to the monster we created. A flicker of fear goes through me. But this time, the wave is under control. Lulu sends it beneath the piece and neatly flips it over.

Lifeboats bob to the surface. But some of them shudder and start to slide beneath the surface.

"Oh, no," I gasp.

"Let me," Dana says, raising her hands. The water turns thick, like lotion. Every boat floats easily to the surface. Lulu summons several small waves to turn the lifeboats over.

"It's working," I say. At some point Evan and I take each other's hands again. I'm clinging to him so tightly I wonder if I'll leave a bruise.

"We need to get everyone into the lifeboats," Evan says.

"Where did Nari go?" I ask. I look around for her familiar long black hair.

"There," Evan says, pointing. "Let's go and help."

I can see Nari in the distance, on the other edge of the wreck. She's carrying a small child in one arm, and her eyes are squeezed tight.

Why does she have her eyes closed? I wonder as I head towards her.

We swim into the middle of a knot of people. Most of them are wearing life jackets. They are clinging to each other and to bits of the ship. Their voices still call for help and for their loved ones. Some are sobbing. Others are wailing. I know that as long as I live, I will never forget the sounds.

A trail of pink streams past me. Blood in the water. I reach out, my hands snagging a tiny wrist. I pull a little boy to me. His dark hair is plastered to his face. His eyes are closed, and his breathing is shallow. Blood gushes from a deep cut in his side.

"Oh, no," I murmur.

I balance the boy on my hip and tear off his life jacket. His green T-shirt has the name Max printed on it. I think about the man calling out for Max.

Without thinking, I place my hands on the boy's side. He's so tiny that my hand covers the entire cut. I calm my breath and channel my healing power into him.

Skin knits itself together under my hand. I hear a gasp. When I open my eyes, Max's dark eyes are open.

"Are you a princess?" he asks.

I laugh in spite of myself. "No, sweetie. I'm more like a fairy godmother."

Max's eyes drift shut. His cut is healed. I swim over to a lifeboat and place him gently over the side. There are people inside, but no one notices me. Then I swim back to the others in the water.

Evan is looping an arm around an old man. With his other hand, he grabs a young woman. He starts pulling them towards the lifeboats. Dana and Lulu are already sending the boats towards us, and they meet us halfway.

I look around again for Nari. She's putting the child into a boat. Other hands reach for the boy, who is sobbing for his dad.

"We'll never get them all," Evan says, glancing over his shoulder.

He's right. There are enough boats, but there are so many people. I don't think it's possible we'll get all of them into a boat before they drown.

But then I blink. *Am I seeing things?* I wonder. *Or are all of the people floating to the boats themselves?*

"Clever, Nari," Lulu says, joining me.

Before I can ask what she means, we both grab the elbows of a young woman and hoist her into the boat. A little girl is next, her eyes wide with terror.

"It'll be okay," I promise as I lift her into the boat. Something bumps my leg. I look down and realize what Nari has done.

"She called the dolphins," I say. A pod of dolphins moves around the survivors, herding them towards safety. That's why she had her eyes closed. She keeps them closed when she's using her powers.

"Keep going," Lulu says. Her arms reach for a stout man. "Keep going."

CHAPTER 8

We don't stop until every last person is inside a lifeboat. Most people look shocked. The water is cold, and everyone is soaking wet. Even though it is summer, it's chilly on the water. They could freeze to death if the wind picks up.

Nari directs the dolphins to push all of the boats together. I feel glimmers of hope as people are reunited. The man who was calling for Max is still saying his name, but now the little boy is curled on his dad's lap. The man says *Max* over and over, as if it's a prayer.

The woman screaming for her babies is also holding them tight, a boy and a girl who are about ten or eleven. The youngest child, a toddler, has fallen asleep on her grandmother's shoulder.

A few people cry in pain, holding arms or even legs at odd angles. They probably have broken bones. Almost everyone is cut or scraped somehow. The water is still faintly pink from blood.

I want to help them the way I helped Max. I know I could heal them. But they're all in boats. I can't risk them seeing us.

Even as we float there, no one notices us. I think they are too much in shock. At least I hope so. Not that I want anyone to be hurt, but I don't want them to realize that mermaids saved them.

My friends and I hover beneath the surface.

"We have to get them to shore," I say.

"I'm on it," Lulu says. She summons a current and sends it towards shore. The boats knock together as they begin to move. Nari sends the dolphins with the boats. We all trail behind.

"Where's Dana?" I ask.

"She went to see what's happening with the wave," Lulu says.

"Oh," I say. "I forgot about the wave."

"We're going to be in so much trouble," Nari says.

I turn to her. "We saved these people. They would have died without us. You did the right thing."

Nari shakes her head, but Lulu is the one who answers. "You don't understand, India. We're the ones who caused the problem in the first place."

My head drops. I felt so much relief that we saved the tourists. I forgot for a moment that we're the ones who caused the shipwreck.

"It's my fault," I whisper. "I'm the one who came here in the first place without an invitation. I kept saying how we needed to do something."

"Don't be so hard on yourself," Evan says. "Everyone played a role in this."

"Except you," I say, looking at him. "You didn't do anything to create the wave. And you jumped in to help right away. Unlike the others."

Evan looks embarrassed. "You had to convince me too. I didn't want to help right away either."

"Why not?" I demand. "How was it even a question for any of you? People were hurt. We needed to help."

Nari turns red. Evan won't meet my gaze.

Lulu sighs. "That's the thing, India. It was people. Not mer." She gestures overhead to where the boats bob, making their way to shore. "If any of them saw our tails..." Her voice trails off. "We risked our lives today. And not just *our* lives – the lives of all of the mer. If humans found out we existed, they would never leave us alone."

I don't have an answer to this. I know the mer need to be kept secret. But I can't imagine not helping the tourists on the shipwreck.

Dana swims up to us, halting the conversation.

"I followed the path of the wave," she says.

"And?" Lulu asks.

"We're okay," Dana answers. "It lost power when it hit the ship. It turned away from shore to the open water. I think it will continue to lose power."

"What about the fish?" Nari asks. "The ones who were in the wave?"

Dana looks pained. "Most of them died."

Her words hang between us.

Better the fish than the humans, I think. I can't say that out loud. I don't want to think that humans are more important than fish. Or more important than the mer. But if I had to pick, I'd pick humans over fish. The mer would probably say this is why the oceans are so polluted.

Evan interrupts my thoughts. "Look," he says, pointing to the surface.

We see shadows overhead. The shadows are boats, all heading towards the lifeboats.

"They're being rescued," I breathe.

"Looks like fishing boats, mainly," Lulu says. "A few lobster trawlers."

I look at Lulu in disbelief.

"What?" she asks.

"How do you know what a lobster trawler is?" I ask. "I barely know what they are."

Grandpa had pointed out the lobster fishing boats in the harbour near his cottage.

Lulu shrugs her shoulders. "Know your enemies," she says.

The words hurt. "I'm not your enemy," I whisper.

"Of course not." Lulu sighs. "I meant humans in general. We gather as much information as possible about their ships. Just in case any of them get too close to the canyons."

"Makes sense," I sniff.

Dana and Nari don't say anything. I suspect they aren't sure whose side to take. I feel a divide opening up between my friends and me. I remember how they weren't sure about helping the humans after the shipwreck. Maybe I will always be too human for them.

Evan takes my hand. His fingers are warm and strong around mine. "We trust you," he says.

I lean closer to him and let my head fall onto his shoulder. "Thanks," I say.

We stay like this until all of the passengers have been lifted from lifeboats onto the decks of sturdier ships. The fleet heads towards shore.

"Look," I say. "We did it."

The words are barely out of my mouth when there's a rush of water behind us. We all turn at the same time and see two dozen Ice and Fire Canyon mer bearing down on us. Ani and Storm lead the pack. The guards who threatened me earlier aren't far behind.

"Uh-oh," I say. I press myself tighter against Evan.

"We've got trouble," he says.

Someone takes my other hand. I look over and see that Lulu, Dana and Nari have joined us. We stand together. Even so, I can feel everyone trembling as the angry mob of mer reach us.

CHAPTER 9

"How could you be so foolish?" Ani shouts as she whirls around her cave. "Of all of the dangerous things you girls have done, this is the worst. The worst!"

Ani has been yelling for what seems like hours. After meeting us at the shipwreck location, the mer took us back to the canyons. A dozen Fire Canyon mer peeled off with Storm and Evan. The Ice Canyon mer went with us to Ani's cave. I can't see the entrance from here, but I bet most of them are still out there, listening to the yelling.

"And all of this for a stupid game?" Ani demands.

We all hang our heads. Lulu, Dana, Nari and I are all in a line, slouched as close to the stone wall as possible. I think we all wish the wall would open up and swallow us whole.

"Answer me!" Ani spits.

We all glance at each other. No one wants to be the first to speak. Ani glares at us, her arms crossed. Nari caves first.

"We ... we thought it would be fun," she whispers.

"You thought it would be fun," Ani says. Her voice is so icy that I shiver.

I can't take it anymore. "It was my fault," I say.

"Go on," Ani says, nodding at me.

"I'm the one who added my healing power to the wave. For some reason, it turned into a monster wave," I say. "I'm not sure how."

"You used your gift on something that didn't need it," Ani says. "That's why it went out of control. You messed with the natural order of things."

I hang my head. "I know," I say.

Ani swims closer to me, ducking to look into my face. "You came here uninvited," she says.

I hang my head further. "I know that too," I say.

"You upset the natural order of things by coming here without being summoned," Ani says.

Tears are streaming down my face, mixing with salt water.

"Mum, India did not mean to cause trouble," Lulu says.

"We're just as much to blame as India," Dana pipes up.

"If you punish her, you have to punish all of us," Nari says. She links her hand in mine.

Ani sighs. "Girls, I admire how you stand up for each other. And you're right – you're all to blame. You all used your powers without need." She looks at me, her eyes narrowed. "But India came here without being called. And it started this whole mess."

It's as if I know what's going to happen before it does. "Please," I beg.

Ani shakes her head. "India Finch," she says, "you are no longer welcome in Ice Canyon."

I've never been punched, which I know is a good thing. But I can imagine that getting punched in the stomach hurts less than what I feel right now. My friends gasp and form a circle around me.

"Please don't," I beg. "I love it here. I love all of you."

"Don't do this, Mum," Lulu says.

"Let her stay," Dana pleads.

"Yes, please, India needs to stay," Nari says.

Ani shakes her head. "My mind is made up."

I'm crying so hard I can't talk.

"But it wasn't just her fault!" Lulu cries. "We all played a part."

"Oh, I know," Ani says. "And you will all be punished as well. But India can no longer come here."

"But what about her healing powers?" Lulu demands. "We need her."

Ani purses her lips. For a moment I think she'll let me stay.

"If we have serious injuries or illnesses, we'll consider calling you. But you will only be brought here to heal," she adds. "We'll keep you under guard at all times. That's all. No hanging out with your friends."

My shoulders shake from my sobs.

Ani lifts her hand as if she's about to lay it on my cheek. At the last minute, she drops her hand without touching me.

"You're just like your father," she says.

I snap to attention. "My dad? What does he have to do with this?" I get chills. Am I finally going to learn why my dad never told me that we were part-mer? Or why he left the ocean and never returned?

Ani looks as if she's trying to make up her mind about something. I see the moment when she decides to tell me.

"I knew your father quite well," Ani finally says. "It was a long time ago. He used to visit."

"What happened?" I ask.

"What has he told you?" Ani asks.

"Nothing. He didn't even tell me about being part-mer. Grandpa was the one who told me everything," I say.

"What does your grandfather know about your dad?" Ani asks.

"All we know is that something bad happened the last time my dad visited," I reply. "Someone got hurt?"

I know there has to be more to it than that. Grandpa and I both heard the rumour that a mermaid died, but I've always hoped it wasn't true.

"I liked Jamal," Ani says. "He was kind and funny. Always telling us stories about living on the land."

This doesn't sound like my dad at all. My dad is kind, but he doesn't talk much. "He's not as talkative now," I say.

"That does not surprise me," Ani says. "Not after what happened."

"What did happen?" Nari asks. My friends are as spellbound by the story as me.

"He fell in love. With a mermaid named Nahla," Ani says. "She was my best friend."

"Then what?" Dana asks.

The question brings Ani back to the present. "Then she died."

"But how?" I persist. "Was it my dad's fault?"

Ani's eyes are sorrowful. I feel as if she's about to give me a heavy burden. "Yes, India."

"What happened?" I ask.

"They went swimming near the Breakers," Ani says. "I believe you know it."

The Breakers is a dangerous spot near Fire Canyon. The currents are strong, just waiting to sweep a mermaid into a jagged row of rocks.

"Oh," I say.

"Your dad was showing off, doing tricks to impress Nahla. And she was just as strong willed as Jamal. She started doing tricks too..." Ani's voice trails off. "She got caught by the currents and slammed into the rocks. She was hurt badly."

"Oh," I repeat. There doesn't seem to be anything else to say.

"Your dad tried to save her, but the damage was too great. A rock had punctured her side. She bled to death in his arms," Ani says.

My head spins. I feel sick and sad. Most of all, I feel sorry for my dad, having to live with Nahla's death. I wonder if this is one of the reasons he and my mum are having problems. Maybe he never got over Nahla.

"The Finches are too dangerous for us. This is why you have to go home," Ani says. "True mer know not to show off our powers."

Her words feel like daggers.

"You're saying I'm not really mer?" I ask, my voice breaking.

"I'm saying your human traits put us in danger," Ani says.

"India was the one who insisted we save the humans," Lulu interrupts. "None of us wanted to save them. India did. Sometimes human traits are better than mer."

"And by saving the humans, you risked being seen," Ani says.

"But if we hadn't saved the humans, they would have drowned," Lulu protests. She swims up to Ani, her eyes wide. "None of us wanted to help. We tried to talk India out of it. But..."

"But?" Ani prompts.

"There were children," Lulu says. "Mums and dads. Babies. Little kids. Grandparents. All of these families. Then they were in the water, about to die, because of something we did. So you can be mad at us for the risk, but India acted better than any of us."

"She did save them," Ani says at last. "And perhaps that was the right decision."

"It was!" Nari says.

"They would have died otherwise, Ani," Dana chimes in.

Ani holds up her hand. "But India still has to go." She glances at the entrance to the cave. "Even if I wanted you to stay, India, my tribe would never allow it. They will only see you as the girl who risked our lives."

I'm crying again, huge sobs that make my entire body shake. "Please," I say.

For a moment, Ani looks at me with compassion. Then her face hardens. "Go."

Her word is like the final peal of a bell. Nothing I say will change her mind. And even if she did let me stay, I'd have a tribe of angry mer to face.

My friends surround me, holding my hands.

"I'm sorry, India," Ani says. "The girls and I will take you to the edge of the canyons. But this is the last time you will ever see each other again."

Ani turns and swims out of the cave. My friends and I are crying too much to talk as we follow her.

No one says anything as we swim away. Most of the tribe watches us go, their faces angry. I don't look at anyone.

I hear someone say, "Traitor". I turn my head and see Melody swimming alongside our group.

I stop and tread water. "Are you saying you would have let them drown?" I ask.

Melody looks shocked that I'm speaking to her. "You put us all in danger. A real mer would never have done that."

"Really?" I say. "Then you should know that I wasn't the only one who helped the humans. Lulu, Dana and Nari helped me. Are you saying they aren't real mer?"

Melody narrows her eyes at me. My friends gather behind me.

"That's not the same," Melody says.

"Isn't it?" I ask. "And, oh, by the way. You know who else saved the humans?" I wait a beat, then say his name: "Evan."

Melody gasps a little.

"So, maybe we're the real mer," I say. "Not you."

"Enough," Ani says, tugging on my shoulder. "Go home, Melody." Then she looks at me. "You too, India. Go home."

I hold back my tears. I give my friends one last hug each.

"Fine," I say. As I swim away, I don't look back once.

CHAPTER 10

My first evening at home is terrible. Grandpa starts lecturing me the moment I walk in the door.

"You went to see the mer," he says, "But they had not summoned you. You broke their rules."

"I know," I say, sinking low in my chair.

"And all you left was a short note. 'Dear Grandpa, Went to the canyons. Back later.'" He fixes me with a look. "You went to see the mer, India. This note makes it sound as if you were nipping to the corner shop."

"I'm sorry," I murmur.

He sighs, resting his head in his hands. "I was so worried."

I feel even worse. "I'm so sorry," I whisper. My emotions catch up with me. "I ... I messed up." Sobbing, I collapse in a chair and tell him the whole story.

He's very angry with me. "How could you do that, India? Risking everything? Both mer and human lives?" he says.

"I know," I say. Tears roll down my face.

Grandpa pauses by my chair. His hand lands heavily on my shoulder, squeezing once. Then he goes to make dinner.

"We heard about the shipwreck," Grandpa says. "The news came in over the radio at work."

"What did they say?" I ask.

"An unexpected wave smashed the boat. There were injuries. A few broken bones, but everyone survived," Grandpa says, sliding eggs onto my plate.

I sigh, relieved. "No one died," I say.

Grandpa watches me over the rim of his mug. "Did anyone see you?"

"I don't think so," I say.

Grandpa places his mug down on the table. "You don't think so," he repeats.

"No," I say.

"But it's possible," he says.

I bend low over my eggs. I'm not very hungry. "Yes," I say, the word slipping from me.

"India...," he starts.

"I know, Grandpa," I say. "I messed up. Big time. I wish I'd never gone to see the mer."

"You made a mistake," Grandpa says. "Now let's hope you don't have to pay a steep price."

The next morning, Grandpa bangs on the door of my room. "India? Get up!" he shouts.

I had been dreaming I was back in the ocean with my friends. We had been laughing and playing. Then a huge wave came up and swept my friends away. Grandpa shocked me out of my dream.

"Be there in a minute, Grandpa," I call. I pull a sweatshirt over my head and pull on some leggings.

When I get to the kitchen, Grandpa is at the table. A newspaper lies in front of him. Even from halfway across the cottage I can see the headline: *MERMAID RESCUE!*

"What is that?" I say.

Grandpa pushes the newspaper to me. I skim the story, not believing my eyes. Then I go back to read it again. The article has quotes from several people who were on the ship that sank. They claim that when they were in the water, they saw mermaids. And that the mermaids helped them.

But what's worse is the picture.

"Oh, no," I gasp.

The photo is grainy and blurry. It looks as if it was taken from one of the lifeboats. I can see the tip of the boat and then water. Below the water, very clearly, is a picture of Evan.

The photo shows his back and waist. His strong arms are reaching for a small girl. And his tail is clearly visible.

"Evan," I whisper. I put down the paper. "Do people believe it?"

Grandpa nods. "Well, I stopped by the Lucky Lobster this morning."

"You did?" I ask, distracted by the thought of Grandpa in the tacky bar. It's also a small ship, bowling alley and an Internet cafe. I can't picture Grandpa dodging fake fishing nets and plastic starfish.

"They're the only place with cable television," he says.

"And?" I ask.

"The story is all over the TV," he says. "All of the breakfast shows were reporting on it."

"Were they making fun of it? Or did they think it was real?" I'm hoping they all think it's a joke.

"A few thought it was fake," Grandpa says. "But I also saw seven news vans setting up along the shore."

"Did you talk to anyone in town?" I ask.

"A few," Grandpa says. "Some thought it was real. Others thought it was a joke."

"That's good, then," I say. "Maybe most people will think it's a joke."

Grandpa bangs his hands on the table, making me jump. "Don't you understand, India?" he asks. "It doesn't matter if people think it's true or not. People will come to town. Then they will rent boats and head to sea, hoping to see a mermaid."

"Why can't the mer just stay away from the area until this blows over?" I ask, gripping the edge of my chair. "Won't that work?"

"You don't understand," Grandpa says, his voice quieter now.

"Not really," I say. "I know the mer hate the humans for polluting the oceans. I agree with them. And I know the mer want to remain a secret from humans. But they have the dome to protect them. Humans can't see through the dome. If the mer stay hidden for a few weeks, they'll be fine."

Grandpa sighs and runs a hand through his thinning hair. "I've never told you what happened to my mother," he says.

"Your mother the mermaid?" I ask.

Grandpa nods. "Her name was Camilla." His voice grows distant.

"Camilla," I repeat. I hadn't heard her name before.

"She was smart and funny," Grandpa continues. "She loved swimming in the deep ocean. But she also loved the land. I think she always wished she could swap her tail for legs, at least some of the time."

"How did she meet your dad?" I ask.

Grandpa looks at me as if he's forgotten I was in the room. "My dad used to dive from the same rocks where you dive. He was a strong swimmer. One day he got caught by the currents. My mother rescued him."

"That's romantic," I say.

"They fell in love and had me. My mother mainly stayed near the rocks. She could be close to us that way," Grandpa explains.

"You couldn't live in the water with your mum?" I ask.

Grandpa shakes his head. "I was born with more human traits than mer traits. I could be in the water with her, but it was easier for me to live with my dad. Here, in this cottage," he says, glancing around.

"So what happened?" I ask, a little afraid to hear the rest of the story.

Grandpa's eyes rest on me. "She was discovered," he says.

"What do you mean?" I ask.

"A fisherman found her one morning. Near the rocks. He happened to have his camera with him. He liked taking photos of the sunrise. Instead he took a picture of my mother," Grandpa says.

"What then?" I ask, colour draining from my face.

"My mother shouted for my father. He came running over to her and saw what had happened. He grabbed the camera from the fisherman and smashed it. My mother slid into the sea," Grandpa says, his voice hollow. "I saw her once more. To say goodbye. Then she left forever."

"You mean she abandoned you?" I ask.

"She had to," Grandpa explains. "She couldn't stay near the coast anymore. She left to keep herself safe, but also to keep us safe."

"You never saw her again?" I ask.

My heart is breaking for him. Tears catch at the corner of my eyes.

"No," he says. "Never again."

"But someone must know something!" I say. "I can ask Ani the next time–"

"She died, India," Grandpa says. "A long time ago."

"How do you know?" I ask.

"When I was old enough, I went into the water to find her," Grandpa explains. "I tracked her for months. I crossed the entire ocean three times, following her trail. Turns out she never really left."

"What do you mean?" I ask.

"She stayed near the shore," Grandpa says. "Always far enough away so no one would see her. But close enough to see us."

An uncomfortable silence falls between us.

"What about the fisherman?" I ask.

"He told his story in town. Some believed him. Others didn't," Grandpa says. "But ever since that day, people have thought the Finches were a little bit strange."

"Oh," I say.

"And now you've risked everything," Grandpa says. "If anyone saw the mer, they would search until they found them. If humans start circling the canyon area, the sea life will scatter. The dome will weaken, and the mer will no longer be protected. India, the mer are in grave danger."

Tears start trickling down my face. "I'm so sorry!" I blurt. I grasp for any hope I can find. "But how do we know humans would harm the mer? Maybe they'll respect the mer. And everyone will become friends."

Grandpa shakes his head. "Are the mer human? Or fish? Humans will capture the mer to study them, dissect them, put them in zoos."

"They can't!" I protest. "The mer aren't animals. They are just like humans!"

"Are you sure everyone on land will see it the same way?" Grandpa asks.

Slowly, I shake my head. Some humans might be fine with the mer. But not everyone.

Grandpa puts his head in his hands. "This is a terrible mess, India."

My heart drops to my feet. "I know," I whisper.

"You need to fix it," Grandpa says, his voice muffled by his hands.

"How?" I ask. "I can't undo the photo."

"We'll find another way," Grandpa says. "But you have to fix it."

He's right, I realize. "Will you help me?" I ask.

Grandpa doesn't speak, but he reaches across the table and takes my hand.

I let out a ragged breath, feeling hope. I don't have to do this alone.

"What do we do first?" I ask.

Grandpa raises his head. "We go to Ice Canyon and tell them what's happened."

I stare at him. "I can't," I say. "They banned me."

"I will go with you. To explain. We will only stay for a few minutes. Then we'll come back," he says.

I want to agree. I'd do anything to see my friends again. But it's hopeless.

"We can't," I say. "We'd never find Ice Canyon on our own."

Grandpa frowns. "That is a problem. You said last time one of your friends was waiting for you."

"Yes," I say. I hope Grandpa doesn't ask me which friend it was. I'm not ready to tell Grandpa about Evan yet.

"Will this friend be there now?" Grandpa asks.

"I doubt it," I say. "All of my friends were involved in the shipwreck. I don't think any of them are leaving the canyons soon."

"We still need to tell them," Grandpa says. "They deserve to know."

"I agree," I say.

Grandpa's face clears. "We don't go to the canyons, then," he says. "We go to the site of the shipwreck."

CHAPTER 11

For the second time in a few days, I'm going to dive into the water. I haven't been summoned, but I'm going anyway. But this time I'm not going alone. Grandpa stands with me.

We climb out to the rocks. The beach behind us fills with people. I see some of the news vans in the car park. A few cameras are set up along the shore.

"You weren't joking about the news reports," I say.

Grandpa snorts. "I never joke, India."

"No kidding, Grandpa," I murmur under my breath.

Usually I jump off the top of the rocks. Today Grandpa takes a side path around the bend.

The path is narrow and wet with spray. My feet slip twice. I don't worry about falling into the water, because my mer abilities would kick in. I can see how the path is dangerous to humans, though. No wonder these rocks are off-limits.

"We'll jump from here," Grandpa says, leading me to a ledge. The waves churn beneath us, making loud sucking sounds. The ends of my hair glitter in the sun with saltwater droplets.

I glance over my shoulder. "No one is behind us," I say.

I can't see the beach from here. That's good, since it means no one can see us jump. If they did, the coast guard would come looking for us. We'd have a hard time explaining later why we were safe.

"Let's go," Grandpa says. He looks straight ahead, crouches and then jumps into the water.

A part of me had expected something more formal. Maybe Grandpa would make a speech or something. This is the first time I've ever seen Grandpa in the water, after all. He hasn't been with the mer since he was a boy. Grandpa isn't much for speeches, though.

My toes grip the edge of the rock. I swing my arms, tuck into a crouch and then spring. I sail over the water. The sunlight warms my skin for an instant. Then I plunge into the icy water.

Grandpa waits for me, his white curls untangling in the current. His eyes are grim.

“Ready?” he asks.

“Ready,” I say.

Grandpa kicks his legs, and then we’re off.

We don’t speak much during the trip. I notice Grandpa looking at everything. The lobsters on the ocean floor. The clouds of silver fish overhead. The sleek bodies of dolphins who swim with us for a bit.

I watch Grandpa’s face closely. He looks like someone visiting the house where he grew up. His face is careful and a little sad.

“Are you okay, Grandpa?” I ask, midway through our trip.

“I’m fine, India,” he says, giving a curt nod. He rubs at his eyes. I’m not sure if it’s sand or a few tears.

We swim towards the shipwreck site. Grandpa knows the coordinates. Our plan is to remain below the surface so no boats see us. We are betting on the fact that the mer will be monitoring the site. One of the mer will see us and bring us to Ice Canyon. At least we hope so.

It takes us a few hours to reach the site. The last time I was here, I was busy with the ship, so I didn't really notice what it looked like. A large hill lurks beneath the water, right on the edge of a deep trench. There are loose stones everywhere. I only know we're in the right spot now because of the cluster of boats on the surface.

There are mer hiding near the trench. A few of them head towards us.

"Hi, Bruce," I say as they swim up. I don't recognize the other two guards. I'm glad to see Bruce, the one guard who likes me.

Bruce's rugged face is grim. "India. Sir," he says, addressing us. He doesn't smile.

"My name is Adam Finch," Grandpa says.

"We know," Bruce says. "You're not supposed to be here. Didn't your granddaughter tell you?"

"She did," Grandpa says. "But we have information that the tribe needs to hear."

"We need to talk to Ani," I say. "Then we'll leave. But we just need to see her for a moment."

"Why?" Bruce asks.

"The shipwreck," I begin. "There's a picture. Of one of the mer. Ani needs to know."

Bruce looks at us carefully, his face serious.

"Please," I add.

Bruce sighs and runs a hand through his short grey hair. "All right," he says. "We'll take you to Ani. This is bad news, though."

"We know," I say.

The guards lead us to the outskirts of Ice Canyon. Word of our arrival has spread. By the time we reach Ani's cave, we are being followed by a large group of angry mer.

I can hear whispers and hisses as we pass.

“What are they doing here?” a voice says.

“You’re not welcome,” another murmurs.

I swim closer to Grandpa and slip my hand into his. He doesn’t let go.

“Be brave,” he whispers to me.

We are led into Ani’s cave. She is surprised to see us. “India? What are you doing here?” she asks.

“I have to tell you something,” I say.

Grandpa clears his throat next to me.

“But first, this is my grandpa,” I say.

“Adam Finch,” Grandpa says.

“I know your name,” Ani says. “I knew Jamal. Way back when.”

Grandpa nods. “He spoke of you too. We know we are breaking the rules by being here. I know what India has done and why she was sent away.”

“Then why are you here?” Ani asks.

“We’re here because of the shipwreck. There was a photo taken by one of the survivors. A photo of a mer,” Grandpa says.

Ani's face goes white. "What are you saying?" she asks.

"I'm telling you that humans know about the mer," Grandpa says.

Ani slouches against the wall of the cave. "So they do know," she says. "No wonder all of the boats were gathering."

"Same as in town," I say. "All kinds of news reporters have arrived."

"Who was it?" Ani asks. "In the picture?"

I squirm. I don't want to say the name. "It was Evan," I say. "The picture shows his back and part of his tail."

Ani snaps her eyes to the guards. "Get Storm and Evan. Bring them here."

The guards nod and leave.

"Oh, and send my daughter and her friends to me," she calls after them. Then Ani turns back to us. "So, how are we going to solve this problem?"

My mind goes blank. I was so focused on getting to the mer that I hadn't thought of any solutions.

"Um, I'm not sure," I say.

Ani looks disappointed. "Maybe the others will have something to contribute," she says.

We spend the next few minutes in silence. Ani crosses her arms and swims back and forth in front of the entrance. Grandpa remains still. I bite my nails, which I do when I'm upset.

My friends interrupt the silence. I can hear them coming before they reach the cave.

"India? India's here?" I hear Dana say.

They burst through the opening of the cave. We have a moment when we freeze, staring at each other. Then they swim towards me in a blur. Soon I'm wrapped up in arms and tails, and we're all crying.

"I never thought we'd see you again," Lulu says.

"I'm so happy you're back," Nari says, brushing tears from my face.

"Don't get too happy," Ani warns. "She won't be staying for long."

My friends start to protest. We're interrupted again by another set of visitors.

"What is the meaning of this?" Storm demands. He bears down on me, glaring. "She's not welcome here! Get out now!"

"That's enough," Grandpa says, swimming to float next to me. "Whatever we have to say can be said without anger."

Storm rears back, shocked. It's a funny sight. Storm is massive, all huge muscles and thick arms. Grandpa is slight and slim next to him. But Grandpa doesn't look away, and Storm backs down.

I catch sight of Evan. His shoulders relax when he sees me. Then he shoots across the cave and folds me in his arms.

"I didn't think I'd ever see you again," he murmurs in my ear.

"I wasn't going to let that happen," I say. I'd say more, but Grandpa is right next to me. I turn to introduce them. "Grandpa, this is Evan."

"Nice to meet you, sir," Evan says.

Grandpa looks Evan over and then gives a single nod. I think that means Grandpa approves.

"Enough," Storm says. "I don't even know why we're here. India and her Ice Canyon friends caused this mess. Not us."

"That's not entirely true," Ani says. She turns to me. "Tell him."

"There was a picture," I start. "In the newspaper." Then I remember the mer don't have newspapers. Or photographs. "Do you know what a picture is? Or a newspaper?"

"We've seen your signs," Ani says. "On the edge of the shore. Images of buildings and people."

"And we find bags with drawings and writing on them in the ocean," Dana adds.

"So billboards and plastic bags," I say. "Okay, so a newspaper is a smaller version of a sign. But it has pictures on it. And the paper we found has a picture."

"Of what?" Storm demands.

"It was of one of the mer," I say. "The picture was of Evan."

Everyone is silent. I glance at Evan. His face turns grey.

Storm's eyes close. He turns to his son. "How could you be so careless?"

Evan firms his chin. "I was helping save the humans in the water," he says. "It was the right thing to do."

"The right thing?" Storm thunders. "The right thing would have been to stay away from that girl and her friends in the first place!"

"I'm not going to do that," Evan says, fire in his eyes. "I'm not staying away from India. Or her friends. And if you make me, I'll run away and join Ice Canyon."

Storm looks as if he's gearing up for an even bigger argument. Ani slides forwards and lays her hand on Storm's arm.

"We have bigger issues," she says. She glances at the cave entrance. Two guards swim into the cave.

"More ships," one of them says. "They've been arriving all morning. Now the entire area is covered with ships."

"The site is about half a mile from the canyons," Storm says.

A heavy silence falls around us. I don't regret saving the people in the sinking ship. But I can't escape the fact that my actions brought humans close to the canyons.

"Well, perhaps it's time to leave," Ani says, pressing a hand to her forehead. "Find a new home. I'm not sure we can swim our way out of this one. If only we could. If we did any swimming near the ships, they'd see us. And then they'd know for sure that mermaids exist."

Ani's words rattle around in my head. Like marbles, running into each other. Then there's a clack as the ideas come together. Suddenly I have the beginning of a very crude, very fuzzy plan.

In the quiet, my plan starts to grow. We need to talk it through. Flesh it out. But I know what we should do.

"Everyone," I say. "I have an idea."

CHAPTER 12

"Are you sure this is going to work?" Lulu asks. Her head bobs alongside the fishing boat I'm sitting in.

"Nope," I say, wriggling into my tail.

"How does it fit?" Dana asks.

"It's a little tight," I say, looking down at my legs. Bold purple fabric covers my strong, brown legs. Instead of my feet, I see a wide, flat tail fin.

"It's supposed to be tight, I think," Lulu says. "It will help you swim better."

"This is silly," I say.

"Now you know what it feels like to be a mermaid!" Nari exclaims.

"I do," I say, flapping my feet to make the tail move. "And it feels silly."

I bought the tail yesterday afternoon at the Lucky Lobster. It was the least tacky one I could find. I've already ripped off the sequins and plastic starfish that it had at first.

"Why do people buy mermaid tails?" Dana muses.

I give my fin a flip. "Humans love stories about mermaids," I say. "And they love to dress up. I think this one is mainly meant to wear around the house, though."

A dark head surfaces next to the boat. Evan leans over the side and takes my hand.

"Are you ready?" he asks.

"Yeah, I guess," I say.

Evan takes a longer look at me in my mermaid costume.

Maybe he wishes I was a full mermaid, I think. Doubt stabs my heart. If I was a real mermaid, I could be with my friends – and Evan – all of the time.

"You look silly," he says with a wink.

"That's what I've been telling them!" I say, relief flooding through me.

Evan leans close to whisper in my ear. "I like you better with your legs," he says. I gape at him, and he blushes. "I mean ... not that I'm noticing your legs or anything ... but..."

"Ready to go, India?" Grandpa asks, coming on deck. Evan lets go of my hand.

I adjust the waist of my mermaid suit. "Yes," I say.

Grandpa kneels next to me. "Are you sure you want to do this?" he asks.

"I need to do it," I say. "I have to make things right."

"We wish we could help," Dana says.

"You've got to stay out of sight," I remind them. "But thanks."

"Good luck, India!" Nari calls.

"See you soon!" Lulu says.

My friends back away from the boat. They will stay a mile or so back. No one wants to risk being seen. Evan stays behind for a moment, holding on to the side of the boat.

"Good luck, India," he whispers.

I wish I wasn't sitting in a mermaid costume. Otherwise I'd lean over and hug him. Or maybe kiss him. I can't move well in the tail, though. Instead I stay where I am and wave as he swims away.

"We're clear on the plan?" Grandpa asks.

"I think we're as clear as we're going to be," I say. "We just need to make sure they see me and get some pictures."

As plans go, this one is simple. I'm going to jump into the water in my mermaid costume. I'll swim to the group of boats that have gathered near the shipwreck site. Grandpa will follow me in the boat. People will see me and think I'm the mermaid from the picture. They'll take some photos. Then I'll explain my swimming teacher back in Birmingham suggested I train with a mermaid tail.

It might be a weak plan, but at least it's a plan. I got the idea from Ani. She said the mer couldn't swim near the boats. But she never said anything about a part-human girl swimming near the boats.

So that's what I'm doing. I'll convince everyone that there aren't mermaids. There's just a clueless girl dressed in a mermaid costume, training. Grandpa will explain that he's keeping an eye out for me, and we're training in the area where the ship sank, so of course that photo is of me.

I slide to the edge of the boat. Grandpa helps me over the railing. Butterflies churn in my stomach. *Here goes nothing*, I think.

"You can do it, India," Grandpa says.

In one moment I'm dangling over the waves. Then I'm plunging into the water.

But something feels wrong the instant I hit the waves. I gasp for breath and swallow water. I cough and sputter. My lungs start to burn.

What is happening? Why aren't my lungs changing?

I kick with my legs and remember that they're bound in the mermaid tail. I do a butterfly kick, both legs together. For a second I surface in the water. I draw a lungful of beautiful, salty air.

Then I start to sink.

"Help!" I shout as my head disappears below the waves.

I look around for the boat. Where is Grandpa? My eyes sting, and the water is dark. I have no idea where the boat is, no idea where my friends are.

I kick again, but I'm getting tired. I start to float down into cold darkness.

My mer abilities aren't waking up. I'm going to drown!

I bat my arms and wiggle my legs. But I keep going down.

Suddenly hands are around my shoulders, pulling me up. A strong tail beats near my face. We climb through the water. Finally, we break the surface. I gasp for cool ocean air.

"Thank you," I say, rolling my head to look at my rescuer. I'm expecting it to be Evan or one of my friends. Maybe Grandpa, even, although he doesn't have a tail.

Instead I see a wreath of golden hair, a red mouth and a pair of perfect blue eyes.

"Melody?" I say, pushing away from her arms. Then I start flailing in the water again.

"Idiot," Melody mutters. She grabs me around the waist and tugs. Then she dives beneath the surface and pulls off my fabric tail. As soon as she does, I feel at home in the water again.

Melody surfaces near me and hands me the tail. "You're welcome," she says, rolling her eyes.

"Wait, you saved me?" I ask. "Why?"

Melody rolls her eyes at me again. "I wasn't going to let you drown. Give me some credit."

"Um, thanks," I say. "Seriously. You saved my life. Thank you. But why are you here at all?"

Melody shrugs. "I couldn't let you have all the fun," she says.

"You think this is fun?" I say with a bitter laugh.

"Fine. I thought about what you said ... about helping people," she says.

"And?" I prompt.

"And you weren't entirely wrong," she says.

"You want to help humans?" I ask.

"Not humans," Melody says, shaking her head. "I want to help the mer."

I guess that's a start. I'm about to tell her that, but my words are cut short by the sound of a motor. I can hear shouts over the boat.

"India? India!" Grandpa's voice rings over the waves. He's joined by my mer friends. I can hear all of them calling for me.

"I'm here!" I yell. "Over here!"

The boat swings around and pulls up next to me and Melody.

"What happened?" Grandpa asks. I'm about to answer when I'm swamped by hugs.

"We thought you were dead!" Nari says.

"We lost you in the water," Dana explains. "We were going to follow at a safe distance."

"But then we couldn't see you," Lulu finishes.

Evan doesn't say anything. He just folds me in his arms for a hard, brief hug. He catches sight of Melody at the same time everyone else does.

"Melody? What are you doing here?" Evan asks.

"She saved my life," I say. "I would have drowned."

"What about your mer powers?" Grandpa asks.

"They didn't activate. I think it was the tail. When Melody took it off me, I was fine," I say. "I don't know why."

"Your legs were bound," Grandpa says. "That might have been why."

"You're probably right," I say before changing the subject. "We still have a problem, though. What are we going to do about the picture? We have to get close enough without the boats seeing any of the mer. And I don't think I can swim in this outfit."

Melody turns to me.

"Do you trust me?" she asks.

"I guess," I say.

Then she tells us her plan. We shape it, add to it. It's not perfect. But in the end, it's what we have. It's all we can do to save the mer.

CHAPTER 13

"Ready?" Melody asks about an hour later. She's floating several metres from the boat.

I'm on the boat, wearing my swimming costume. The mermaid tail lies forgotten on deck. "Yep," I say. "And Melody?"

"What?" she asks, glancing back at me.

"Good luck," I say.

She gives me a serious nod and then slips beneath the waves. She disappears. And we wait.

"Do you think this is going to work?" Lulu asks, hanging on to the side of the boat.

Dana is swimming in lazy circles nearby. Evan floats in the water to the port side, right near me.

"I hope so," Dana says. "I don't want to move away."

"Me, neither," Lulu says.

Something bumps the side of the boat.

"We're here," Nari says, poking her head out of the water. A pod of seals follows her.

"You got the seals. Thank goodness," I say, realizing it is one of the stranger things I've ever said.

Grandpa checks his watch. "It's time," he says. "If this plan is going to work, we should see the boats by now."

I stand and shade my eyes. I can see ships moving towards me. Nari turns towards the seals and instructs them to swim between the boats.

Then I hear the music. Melody's voice slides through the waves. I'd follow her voice anywhere. So would the ships. They are all sailing straight towards us. They are all following Melody's voice.

The ships are mainly fishing boats. Some smaller speedboats. Even a lobster trawler or two.

"There they are," Grandpa says. I feel a flash of anger that he interrupted me listening to Melody.

Grandpa pauses to put earplugs in his ears. He hands me a pair. He knew we were too human to listen to Melody's song and came prepared.

"Wait," I say. I try to block out Melody's song. I motion to my friends, who swim over to me.

"We'll send a wreath, no matter what," Lulu promises. "I'll tell my mum she has to invite you back. No matter what the tribe thinks. We need to know what's happening with the humans."

"I'll see you soon, then," I say. My voice cracks and tears form in my eyes.

"Goodbye, India," my friends say, squeezing my hand before they swim away. They'll follow us as far as possible. But I won't get to see them again once we get to land. Maybe not ever again.

Evan is the last to say goodbye. He holds my hand and looks into my eyes. He doesn't say anything. Neither do I.

Then he lets go of my hand and is gone beneath the waves.

I slip my earplugs into my ears. Grandpa starts the motor and swings the boat towards the ones coming towards us. Grandpa steers our boat to the front of the line. I wait for someone to notice us, to call or shout. But no one stops or shouts.

I glance into the cottage of the first ship behind us. I can see the guy driving it. His eyes are glassy, and he doesn't blink.

Grandpa steers the boat north for a while. Then we veer west. Every once in a while, we see an ice blue tail break the surface of the water. Melody, telling us we're on the right path.

A few hours later, we slide into the harbour near home. After we dock the boat, Grandpa motions me to take out my earplugs. Then he gets out his megaphone and turns towards the crowd of boats.

"That concludes our tour, folks," he calls. His voice travels clearly over the water. "Sorry to see no one caught any fish. But we did get a good look at the new seal colony offshore. And look, a bunch of them followed us home!"

There are oohs and ahs from the boats.

"Maybe that's where all the mermaid rumours are coming from," Grandpa says, forcing a laugh.

In the boats around us, the men and women look as if they're waking up from a dream. Some of them look confused. Others look lost. Most of them look blissfully content. Cameras flash as people take photos of the seals.

"You all have a good trip back to your home harbours," Grandpa says. "Thanks for travelling with Finch Tours."

"Do you think it will work?" I ask.

Grandpa nods at the car park of the harbour. Fifteen news vans are waiting. A dozen reporters are heading towards us. "Let's find out," he says. "Wait for me by the bait shop."

Reporters swarm Grandpa and thrust microphones into his face. As I walk past, I hear him talking about his most recent tour of the mermaid site.

"Nope, no one saw a mermaid," he says. "Not that I thought they would. Most mermaid sightings are seals. And there is a new seal colony near the shipwreck site. Look, you can see them yourselves."

He points at the dark heads bobbing in the water. “I’d say that’s what those survivors saw,” Grandpa continues. “They were pretty shaken up. It would be easy to confuse a seal with a mermaid.”

The reporters have more questions, but I can see that some of them look as if they believe Grandpa’s story that he took a group of ships out to look for mermaids. But all anyone saw were some seals.

I glance out across the waters. My friends are out there somewhere. They followed us most of the way. I wonder if they are hiding out there, trying to see me.

The boats Melody led are sailing away. A few are docking here. I duck into the shadows as a man and woman pass me by.

“That was a good tour,” the man is saying. “Too bad we didn’t see any mermaids.”

“I wonder if it really was a seal, Bob,” the woman is saying. “That’s what the tour guide was saying.”

Bob nods. “I think so too, Shelly. By the way, did we pay him?”

Shelly's voice stumbles. "I ... I think it was free. I don't remember. Did he say anything when we signed up for it?"

Bob is shaking his head. "I don't really remember. When did we sign up?"

My breath catches in my throat. Maybe the plan won't work after all.

"We must have signed up today," Shelly says. "I think I got too much sun. My mind is a little hazy."

I don't dare breathe.

"Mine too," Bob says after a moment. "Maybe that's what happened to the survivors too. They got too much sun and thought they saw mermaids."

"Let's go home, honey," Shelly says, following Bob to a blue car.

I let out my breath. I'm hoping everyone in the group of ships feels the same way. As if they don't quite remember what happened. All we need them to remember is what my grandpa told them – it was a seal, not a mermaid.

It was Melody's idea. She said she could lead the boats away and sing long enough so that everyone's memories would be fuzzy.

Grandpa said he and I could help lead the boats somewhere safe. And plant the idea that they were part of a tour that saw nothing but seals.

I wasn't a fan of the plan at first. "They're going to come back," I insisted. "Or someone else will. We've made it a mysterious spot. And people are going to come back again and again."

"That's why we have a second plan," Lulu said.

"What is it?" I asked. Just then, a shudder went through the water.

"Look," Lulu said. She took my arm and pulled me beneath the surface. Below us, several mermaids were building a pile out of rocks. I recognized Shana from our competition at the *Clemmons*.

"What are they doing?" I asked.

"They're building a small island," Dana explained. "Nothing big, just a pile of rocks. Later Nari is going to bring the seals back here. It will look just like a seal colony."

"Huh," Grandpa said. "This might actually work."

"You think?" I pressed.

"We'll just have to wait and see," Grandpa said.

Grandpa's words ring in my mind as I stand in the car park. *Wait and see*. It's not how I like to do things. But I don't really have a choice.

"You okay?" Grandpa asks, coming over to me. The news reporters are milling around, looking bored. I think about my friends. And I think about how close I came to ruining everything.

Suddenly the emotions of the day hit me hard. "Will it always be like this?" I ask, tears falling down my face.

Grandpa puts his hand on my shoulder. "There, there," he says, patting my arm awkwardly. "It will be all right."

"But how do you know?" I ask.

"I don't," Grandpa says simply. "But there's nothing in the world a nice long sleep can't fix. Everything will look better in the morning. Now let's head home."

CHAPTER 14

Over the next few days, Grandpa and I read the newspaper every morning. I go to town every afternoon to watch TV at the Lucky Lobster bowling lanes. When I have a signal, I check my phone for news stories.

Of course, some boats return to the shipwreck site. But all they find is a pile of rocks and a colony of seals. Finally, the newspapers decide the picture must have been faked. So do the TV reporters. They bring in photo experts who say it might have been a seal. The original shipwreck survivors agree they were so confused that they likely didn't see mermaids after all.

Little by little, the news vans and reporters start to depart.

"It's done," Grandpa says a week later.

"You think so?" I ask.

"I do," he says. "The last reporter left town yesterday afternoon. The mer still need to be careful. But I think the danger has passed."

"Good," I say. I can relax for the first time in a long while.

I watch Grandpa potter around the cottage. I remember how he looked in the water at Ice Canyon, as if he couldn't believe he was there.

"Do you miss the mer?" I ask.

Grandpa pauses as he lifts a plate to the cupboard. "It was nice to be back for a visit," he says at last.

"Do ever think about going back more often? Now that Grandma's gone?" I ask. My grandma died before I was born. Grandpa said she was the reason he chose to stay on land.

"I made my choice, India," Grandpa says. "Even though Elaine is gone, I still honour that choice."

"Okay," I say. I don't really understand what he means. But I get the sense I shouldn't ask.

"Besides, the mer are your friends now," he says. "You should go to them."

"They haven't sent a wreath," I say. "And I'm pretty sure Ani is still angry. Not to mention the rest of the tribe."

Grandpa puts one hand on mine and gives it a squeeze. "Go to the shore. See if they've summoned you," he says. "I'll be waiting here."

"Um, okay," I say, getting to my feet. "I'll see you soon, Grandpa."

As soon as I reach the beach, I see the wreath. My friends have called for me. Grinning from ear to ear, I race to the rocks. The beach is empty now that the news vans have left. I check to make sure I'm alone, and then I dive into the waves.

Everyone is waiting for me. Lulu, Dana, Nari. And Evan.

"You're here!" I exclaim. They all smile at me, but their faces are tense. "What's going on?" I ask. "Why do you all look so nervous?"

"Do we still have reason to be nervous?" another voice asks. I look up in surprise as Ani swims up to us.

"Ani," I say.

"India," she replies formally. "Do you have news?"

"Yes, good news," I say. I tell them everything. How the boats are gone, how people think the photo was faked or just a seal.

"That's good," Ani says. "We had hoped as much. The dome protecting the canyon is stronger. And we haven't seen any signs of boats since Melody led them away."

"Did you know she could do that?" I ask. "Make them follow her and erase their memories?"

"Mermaid song has always been very powerful," Ani says.

Lulu fidgets behind her mother. Nari and Dana are floating with linked arms, watching the conversation. And Evan hasn't taken his eyes off me once. I would do anything to be with them again.

"So ... can I come back?" I ask Ani.

"That's the question, isn't it?" Ani says with a sigh.

"Um, I suppose so," I say.

"You put the mer in danger," she says. Then she sweeps her hand to include my friends. "All of you put the mer in danger."

"We're sorry," I say, my voice broken. *She's not going to let me come back,* I think.

"But you also tried to make it better. I can't fault you for that," Ani says.

Hope rises in my chest, like the bubbles in sparkling water. "Does this mean I can come back?" I ask.

Ani pauses.

"Please, Mum," Lulu says.

"Yes, please," Dana adds.

Ani glances at my friends and then back at me. "Well, it seems I've been outvoted," she says. She smiles as she speaks, so I don't think she's too angry with me anymore. "Very well, you can come back to us, India Finch." Her face turns serious. "But only when we call you. And I cannot promise I can protect you from the entire tribe. Do you understand?"

"Yes," I say.

"See you soon, then," Ani says. With a final flick of her tail, she swims away.

My friends give huge whoops of excitement, and we all fall into each other.

"You're back!" Lulu says.

"I'm so happy!" Dana shouts, squeezing my hands.

"Me too," I say.

"Me three!" Nari adds.

Someone taps my shoulder. I turn to find Evan in front of me.

"I'm happy too," he murmurs.

Evan's face dips towards mine. I lift mine to his. Our lips touch as if it's the most natural thing in the world.

I'm blushing when we pull away. So is Evan. My friends watch with their mouths hanging open.

"Um, see you around, India," Evan says. He turns and speeds away from us.

My eyes are bright when I turn back to my friends.

"So that happened," I say.

My words break the silence. My friends surround me again, everyone talking at once. Soon we are deep in conversation about what it all means.

The ocean is beautiful and warm. I'm with my friends. The boy I like just kissed me. And I have a home again with the mer. I don't know if it will always be my home. And I don't know if the mer will always be safe. But for now, they are safe. I'm home. In this moment, all is right.

ABOUT THE AUTHOR

Although **Julie Gilbert's** masterpiece, *The Adventures of Kitty Bob: Alien Warlord Cat,* has sadly been out of print since Julie last stapled it together in the fourth grade, she continues to write. Her short fiction, which has appeared in numerous publications, explores topics ranging from airport security lines to adoption to antique wreaths made of hair. Julie makes her home in southern Minnesota, USA, with her husband and two children.

ABOUT THE ILLUSTRATOR

Kirbi Fagan is a vintage-inspired artist living in the Detroit, Michigan, area, USA. She is an award-winning illustrator who specializes in creating art for young readers. She received her bachelor's degree in illustration from Kendall College of Art and Design. Kirbi lives by two words: "Spread joy". She is known to say, "I'm in it with my whole heart". When not illustrating, Kirbi enjoys writing stories, spending time with her family and rollerblading with her dog, Sophie.

GLOSSARY

churns to move roughly

compassion concern for someone in trouble that leads to the desire to help that person

generation all the members of a group of people or creatures born around the same time

harpoons spears with barbs that are jabbed, fired or thrown at a target

heritage property or traditions that are handed down from ancestors

legacy qualities and actions that one is remembered for; something that is passed on to future generations

lobster trawlers large boats that drag nets through the water to catch lobsters

shudder to shake or tremble violently

summon to request or to order that someone come or appear

survivors people who live through a disaster or horrible event

FURTHER DISCOVERIES

1. The mer only summon India when she's needed. What do you think this says about her friendships with the mer?

2. Compare what the mer do on a normal day to what you do on a normal day. Which life sounds more appealing to you? Why?

3. We learn what happened when India used her healing power on something that did not need healing. What do you think would happen if she used the power on a mer or human who didn't need it? Explain your answer.

4. India says she would pick saving humans over saving fish. Do you think the mer would agree?

5. Now that India knows more about what happened with her father and the mer, do you think she will talk to him about it? What would you do if he were your father?

6. India's grandpa hadn't swum with the mermaids since he was a boy. How do you think he felt about returning to the water?

WRITING INSPIRATION

1. Some of the mermaids' powers are described in this book. Of the ones described, which of the powers would you most like to have and why? Use details from the book to support your answer.

2. When Ani decides that India can stay, she mentions that India can help heal jellyfish stings. Use details from scenes where India uses her healing powers to write a new scene of her healing the stings.

3. There are many legends about Sirens, mermaids with the power to hypnotize humans. Research these stories and write a retelling of one in your own words. Or write your own original Siren story.

4. Write a newspaper article about the shipwreck, using details from the text. Include quotes from characters mentioned in the book.

5. Pretend you are India, just back from being banished from the canyons. Write a journal entry about your feelings and worries. Then write a journal entry about what happens at the conclusion of the book.

JOURNEY EVEN DEEPER INTO...

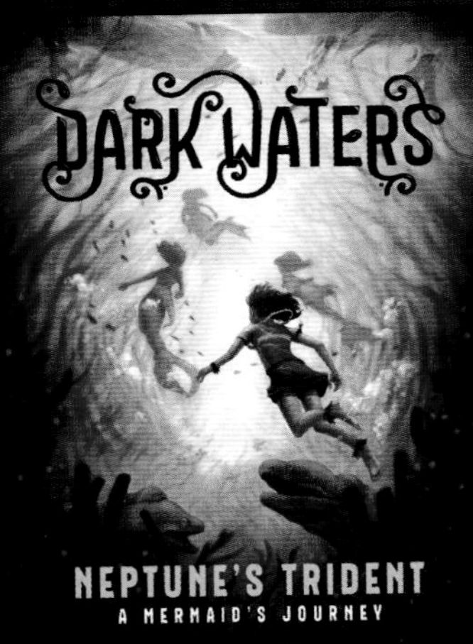

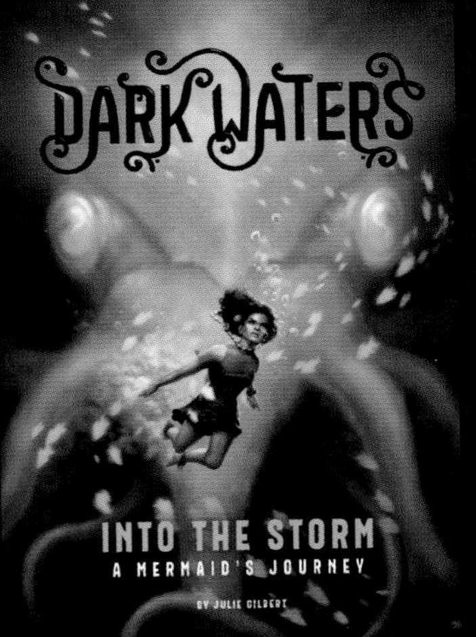